DAWN OF THE JAGUAR

TERRY SPEAR

PUBLISHED BY:

Wilde Ink Publishing

Dawn of the Jaguar

Copyright © 2021 by Terry Spear

Cover Copyright by Covers by Julie

Discover more about Terry Spear at:

http://www.terryspear.com/

Print ISBN: 978-1-63311-077-9

Ebook ISBN: 978-1-63311-076-2

SYNOPSIS

Erin Chambers is leaving the FBI to join her father in his Big Cat Private Investigations Agency. She loved her job, but she wants to be closer to her father and have more freedom to run as a jaguar shifter when she can. But she knows dealing with her dad's sole private investigator, Jason Biggerstaff, is going to take some work. He's a hot jaguar and turns up the heat whenever he's around her without any effort at all, to her consternation. But he's not fond of the FBI, and she and he butt heads all the time. He's been like a son to her father, so she knows he was thinking he could take over the business one day. That's not happening.

Jason Biggerstaff is busy with investigations, not thrilled that Erin is joining the agency, but all that changes when they are embroiled in missing kids' cases, their usual run-of-the-mill investigations, and she's really good at her job. No matter how much he fights the attraction he has for her, it's a losing battle. What starts out as just them handling their usual cases, turns into something worse—a shifter in trouble and they must save him without landing themselves in a worse mess than they already are, which includes dealing with this growing need to take their relationship to something they never bargained for.

Thanks so much to Alison Bratton for loving my books! And thanks for being such a good Facebook friend and sharing my work with others. You always cheer me. Your comment, "I have every one of your print book and ebooks. I love all the shifters series, so please keep writing."— made my day! And thanks for helping others in their time of need before retiring as a Registered Nurse. You are a hero.

CHAPTER 1

The winter wind whipped around the Big Cat Private Investigations Agency building situated in a wooded area of The Woodlands, near Houston, Texas when private investigator Cannon Chambers got a call, spoke on the phone, and then ended the call, and waved to Jason Biggerstaff. Jason really liked the retired police detective who owned the jaguar shifter run PI agency. Cannon had hired him to be his investigator three years ago and Jason wouldn't have wanted to be anywhere else after he left the police force where he had worked previously. But the situation at the job was dramatically changing at the agency in about an hour, only three days into the new year.

Cannon's only surviving daughter, an FBI agent, was joining the business. Jason had seriously thought of finding another investigative agency to work for when that happened because he and Erin didn't see eye-to-eye about anything. Eventually, Cannon wanted his daughter to take over the business and then Erin would be running things. Even worse.

"I've got a client coming in shortly," Cannon said.

"Okay." Usually they didn't have clients who specifically asked for one or the other of them and Jason often went through the cases first to pull the ones for Cannon he knew he preferred to handle.

Jason owed it to her father to continue investigating cases for him as long as he could. Not to mention he loved working at a jaguar run office, especially after he had been raised in foster care by humans who'd had no knowledge of what he was. Cannon had treated him like a son and Jason had even had the far-out notion that Cannon might someday give the business to him because he hadn't been sure Erin was ever going to give up her FBI job and join them. Now, she had resigned her position at the FBI as a field agent and had wrapped up whatever she had needed to do there and was returning home today—for good. If things got too bad between Jason and Erin, he was out of there.

He'd been working on a bunch of background security checks for some potential new employees at a nursing home and then he was looking into a case of a runaway teen. Normally, he was focused totally on his work, but he couldn't help thinking about Erin and how she was going to turn things upside down at the office. He hoped not. But she was strong-willed and so was he, so he could see them butting heads.

Cannon walked out of his office where Jason was working at his desk. Across the room was Erin's desk. It had never been filled. It was just sitting there, waiting for her to come to work and had been for three years. Except for the cleaning service dusting it off daily, no one touched it. Jason knew Cannon had wanted his daughter to leave her job sooner, but he also knew she had to do what she felt she needed to before she gave it up. Jason didn't blame her. He would have felt the same way as her.

While he was searching for any criminal records on the employees, he found one had ten outstanding driving violations and he flagged it. He wasn't doing the hiring, so all he did was hand over the information to the personnel manager of the organization who was paying for their services, and she would decide which employees were all right to hire, and who might be a risk.

If it were him, he'd seriously consider all the driving violations. Those were just the ones officers had caught her at. What else had she done that she had gotten away with?

Everyone else looked fine, so he typed up his report and sent it to the personnel manager who immediately responded, thanking him. He could follow up on the case, just to see who was hired, but there was no need, so he let it go. Once he had given the office the report, it was out of his hands.

Next, he had to look into the situation of the runaway teen. It had happened so many times before that no one even worried if the boy was in trouble any longer. The boy who cried wolf came to mind. Jason had found him twice already, so it was just another one of those days. He pulled up his file on the teen and looked through the notes he had on where he'd found him before, who all his friends were, where he normally hung out. The kid had a great home life—as far as he knew—devoted parents, a nice home, everything he could ask for, but he liked the drama of running away and being on the lam and then being found. Jason just hoped that he would always be found safe and sound. The kid was foolhardy to believe he would always be safe. There were a lot of bad people out there.

So many kids didn't have half of what the boy had. Some came from broken homes, a parent, or both, sitting in jail, bad neighborhoods, no one to mentor them. Jason had really needed a jaguar mentor while growing up. When he'd lost his parents, he'd had to live in foster care, and he had been a runaway. But he'd had a good reason too. As a jaguar shifter, he had hated to be confined to a home, a regimen, a world that didn't understand him. He hadn't been a good kid growing up. He'd only survived because he was a big cat, and he had a fighting spirit that rivaled any human kid's. Or adult's, for that matter.

Somehow, he'd managed to survive those tumultuous years, but he always shook his head at the kids who had everything and acted like they were so put upon, when he'd had virtually nothing. He'd even counseled the teen about his behavior, but he could tell his talks went in one ear and out the other. The teen had just been lucky he hadn't been hurt while he was running around wild.

A woman walked into the office and Jason greeted her. "How may I help you?" That was his other duty as assigned—the receptionist for the agency. They'd had one two years ago, but she'd had a drinking problem and wasn't filing papers correctly, calling in sick, sleeping at the desk when Jason and Cannon were out doing surveillance, and finally Cannon had had enough and fired her. Jason would have done it much earlier than Cannon had. Jason didn't have a lot of tolerance for people who didn't pull their own weight. He guessed it was because he had to finally pull himself up by the bootstraps and work hard to make something of himself. He didn't have any use for people who threw their lives away for nothing.

The woman who had walked into their agency was a blond, her eyes olive green like a cat's, and she appeared to be in her mid-fifties. She was looking at the certificates on the wall and then she glanced at him. "I'm looking for a PI to investigate a man who has been stealing from my bank account. I spoke with Cannon about it." Jason smelled her scent and realized she was a jaguar shifter like them, unless she worked at a zoo in the big cat's enclosure, which he highly doubted.

"I've got it," Cannon said, eager to meet with the woman, practically racing out of his office as if Jason might steal the case from him. Cannon didn't often grab a case before Jason had a look at it, but Cannon loved cases like this, having been a police detective before he retired and had worked a branch of financial fraud cases prior to starting the PI agency. He'd actually started it because his wife had been a PI, working for an unreasonable boss and when Cannon had fallen hard for her, he had used his savings to set her up in the practice of her own and joined her once he had the training and qualifications too. The car accident that had killed her and Erin's twin brother had been a real travesty, but in memory of his wife and son, Cannon continued operating the agency because it had been his wife's lifelong pursuit and then he had hired Jason to take up the slack.

All smiles, Cannon welcomed the client into his office, shaking her hand in a more than familiar way. "I'm Cannon Chambers and I worked as a financial fraud investigator for a number of years." Then he shut the door to have a private consultation with his client.

Smiling, Jason shook his head. He'd never seen Cannon mix pleasure with business. If the woman was single, who knew where things might lead.

Jason made a few calls to see if he could locate the teen and then learned he'd been picked up by the police for stealing a thirty dollar-pen from an office supply store. Jason made a courtesy call to the parents, and they were devastated, naturally, after having heard from the police already. Some people just had a propensity for self-sabotage. Early in life, so did Jason. He had been so angry that his parents had been taken away from him that he had wanted to take it out on the whole world. At some point, a police detective had talked to him about it, told him he was going to end up in jail if he didn't see the light. And that made him want to be a police officer, to help kids in need, if he could reach them. He'd done pretty well at it in the past, both as a police officer and in this job. But this kid? Well, Jason didn't want to call him a doomed case because there was always the possibility that someone could turn themselves around.

He just hoped it was sooner than later.

Then the lady left Cannon's office, not looking any happier than she did when she had walked into the office, and Jason hoped she hadn't decided Cannon couldn't do anything for her.

But then Cannon came out of the office, smiling as she left the building. "You'll need to pick up Erin at the airport in an hour."

"I thought you were going to do that." The words were out of

Jason's mouth before he could stop them. Erin had been so looking forward to seeing her dad, she was going to love it if Jason picked her up instead. *Not.*

"I have this case to work on. What about yours?" Cannon looked at the runaway teen's file on his desk, his inbox empty.

"All taken care of."

"That's what I like about you. You're not sitting around waiting to get a paycheck. You earn it."

"That kid got picked up by the police."

"Timothy Benton? We knew it was going to happen sooner or later. So are you going to pick up my daughter at the airport?"

"Yeah, sure."

"Good. I need to make a trip to the bank and then I've got a lunch engagement."

"With Erin," Jason reminded him, in case Cannon had forgotten he had planned to welcome Erin to the agency properly by taking her out to lunch while Jason took care any of the cases that arose here. Though he took work-related calls on his phone anywhere at any time.

"Uh, with a client. You take Erin out to our favorite spot. I'm going to a different place."

Jason raised a brow.

"Strictly business. The client believes the manager of the Seafood and Steak Alehouse is stealing from her bank account."

"So you have to eat with her there?" That was a new one on Jason.

"Yeah. Anyway, tell Erin you'll take her to lunch once you pick her up from the airport. I'm off to the bank."

Jason watched as Cannon slipped out of the office with a spring in his step. He wasn't sure how Erin would take being stood up by her father because he'd gotten interested in a she-cat client. Unless Jason was totally off the mark, but he didn't think so. Big cats had an extraordinary sense of smell and they sensed things humans might oversee. There was more to this case than just learning about stolen funds from the woman's bank account.

He hadn't believed the woman had known Cannon before this, but maybe she had. It appeared she had never been to the office, didn't know Cannon had a separate office, and so she had taken a moment to orient herself when she walked into the agency. He also would have smelled her scent in here before.

Jason wasn't about to tell Erin why her father didn't come for her though. He would let Cannon explain it to his daughter if he was getting interested in a client. That had never happened in or out of the office since Jason had known him. So maybe he was mistaken.

He just had to remember to pick up Erin at the airport on time or she would be all bent out of shape, more so than she probably already was. As far as lunch went, he figured he'd leave it up to her as to whether she wanted to have lunch with him or not, like he usually did with her father. Hopefully, Erin would have other plans that didn't include Jason.

CHAPTER 2

*E*rin Chambers got a call from Jason Biggerstaff, the man who worked for her dad at the Big Cat Private Investigations Agency. Wishing she could have had a direct flight from Bethesda, Maryland, she was now at the airport waiting to fly out from Dallas to Houston, Texas after leaving the FBI to join her dad at his agency. The biggest problem she figured she was going to have when she started working at the agency was dealing with Jason. Otherwise, she was looking forward to beginning working at the family business.

"Yeah, Jason?" She knew he was supposed to pick her up at the airport instead of her dad because he had texted her that he was working on an important case. Not that Jason probably wasn't also, but she suspected her dad was trying hard to push the two of them together so they would at least like each other.

It wasn't happening.

"I don't know why Dad wanted you to come and pick me up. I can manage on my own. I can always take an Uber or taxi." She didn't need her "partner" at the agency to come pick her up.

"Your dad asked me to pick you up so that's what I'm doing. It's always a contest between us. Just take the gesture as—"

"My father's order."

"Fine. I'll wait for you at the baggage claim."

"Yeah, sure, thanks." She wanted to tell him he didn't need to park the car and could instead just wait in the line of cars for arrivals. She could manage her own bags. Well, somehow. She figured if she'd said so, he'd believe that was a further "contest of wills," but she really just felt he didn't need to pay for short-term parking since she'd be out of the airport before he even knew it.

She hoped they could work together well, and it wouldn't always be an argument between them, but she knew he didn't care for FBI agents in general, and she figured he had also wanted to take over the business when her father retired. Not that that would happen any time soon. Her father treated Jason like the son—her twin brother—he'd lost, as much as he was always telling her all the great cases Jason had solved. If she was being honest with herself, that bugged her more than she wanted to admit.

Of course her father didn't know about all the cases *she'd* solved as an FBI agent, except for the couple of times she was a lead investigator and ended up being in the news.

Jason was actually more by the books than she ever was, and he didn't like that she wasn't. Sometimes she found bending the rules got her results much faster. He might not like the idea of working for a woman either. She knew he was totally dedicated to her dad, but he was also great at his job, so she wanted to keep him on if he'd work with her. She wasn't dictatorial in her leadership and generally, she could get along with anyone. She had gone into the FBI and learned all she could there so when she was able to work with her dad, she would have a good investigative background. She had hoped she would complement Jason's police investigative training, but she wasn't sure if their personalities would just clash instead.

When she finally arrived at the airport and made her way to the baggage carousels, she saw Jason already standing there looking at his phone, texting someone. His shaggy black bangs were windswept across his forehead, his eyes as dark as dark chocolate, a trim beard and moustache giving him a sinfully rugged appearance. He was dressed in khaki pants and a black turtleneck, no leather jacket this time. But she was wearing hers now that she was no longer with the FBI. She loved that aspect of her job. She could wear what she wanted that she felt was appropriate to the mission.

She walked up next to him, breathing in his hot, jaguar scent brushed by the wintry breeze and all sexy male before she let him know she was there. She was surprised he hadn't turned to see her already, but she wondered if he was putting on an air of disinterest and knew very well she was in his space. Or he was texting a hot date? "Waiting for someone?"

Jumping a little, he nearly dropped his phone and swung his attention around to look at her. "Hell, you're early."

She wanted to laugh. So he hadn't known she was there. "Nice seeing you again too." She hadn't thought she could sneak up on the big cat, as much they were wary of their surroundings, hearing and seeing everything. She turned to watch the motionless conveyer belt, hoping it wouldn't take long to get her bags and hoping her bags hadn't been lost.

"We have a mission to go on. Your dad was just texting me about it."

"He didn't send *me* information about the case." She was surprised her dad had sent it just to Jason and not to her too. She hoped her dad didn't plan to send all the information on cases to Jason so he could relay it to her because she was a new investigator.

"Is your phone on?" Jason asked.

"Yes, of course it is. I already texted Dad to let him know I had arrived at the airport."

"Maybe he sent the text to me, figuring you would be on your way to the baggage claim and not have time to read it. Whereas I was here already, waiting on you."

"Which I appreciate. There's nothing worse than arriving at your destination and having to wait forever on someone to pick you up. So about the case?"

"An eight-year-old boy left his house and vanished. The boy's name is Henry Potter. The police and everyone else are looking into it, they have no leads. Your dad said with our"—Jason looked about to see how close people were standing to them—"with our enhanced cat senses, we could possibly find him when no one else can. Time is of the essence." He showed her a picture of the blonde-haired boy with bright blue eyes and the sweetest smile.

The conveyer belt began to move, and she was ready to pounce on her bags as soon as she spied them so they could get on the road. Feeling antsy that this could be a life-or-death matter and getting the bags could take too long, she said, "We could come back for the bags later. Oh, wait, there my bags are. The three jaguar print ones." She was glad that most everyone else's bags were black. No one else had jaguar print ones, at least that had come out on the belt, and she recognized them from all the scrapes and gauges they'd suffered from previous plane trips. She didn't understand how luggage being tossed on a plane could make it appear that her bags had had to fight for their lives.

She rushed forward to grab one and was surprised to see Jason grab the other two heavier ones practically at the same time. She couldn't have managed. "Thanks."

"Is that all of them?"

"Yeah. Is my dad working on the case and that's why he didn't pick me up?" She assumed he would be because it had to be high priority. She also figured this hadn't been a way for him to just throw her and Jason together like she'd earlier thought. And she was glad for that.

* * *

"A CLIENT HAD WALKED in right before he was supposed to come and pick you up and so he said he had to handle the case and asked me to get you instead," Jason said to Erin as they rolled the bags toward the doors leading out to the parking tower. "Then he just texted me about this new case that we're taking on. The clients are Henry's parents, who don't believe the police are searching in the right direction and didn't want to wait until it was too late. So your dad didn't know about the new case before he asked me to come get you. I'm sure Cannon wants to get involved in it, given the seriousness of it." When Erin had slipped up next to Jason, startling the crap out of him—which was not easy for anyone to do since he was usually a hell of a lot more alert than that—he hadn't remembered how pretty she was. Or how fragrant her big she-cat scent was—like roses, and cool breezes, sugar, and cinnamon.

Beautiful, dark brown hair with golden streaks highlighting it, catlike amber eyes that fairly glowed in the bright lights of the baggage claim area, her black leather pants formfitting to her shapely legs, high heeled black leather boots adding to her petite height, a black leather jacket and a black shirt that revealed the slight swell of her breasts added to the appeal. Though none of that changed anything about the way she rubbed him the wrong way.

No way was Jason going to tell her what he suspected—that the woman who had come to see Cannon had more to do with him than being a client needing help with a case, if what he suspected was true. But what if he was wrong? He certainly didn't want to say something about it if he was way off base. "You do know how much your dad loves financial fraud cases, right? When the woman—" he meant to say client, *damn it*—"came in, he took the case right away."

"Woman? The way you said woman makes me wonder—is she *his* age? A she-cat?" Erin frowned at him.

Jason should have known Erin would have suspected something more was going on because her dad normally would have given the case to Jason and picked up his daughter at the airport. She'd been daddy's little girl forever.

"Well?"

"Yeah, on both counts."

"Okay, well, at least he's still having lunch with me and I'm sure that's why he wanted to get started on this case right away so he and I could discuss it."

"About that—" So much for Jason not telling her all that was going on!

Erin narrowed her eyes at him as they headed outside to the parking garage. He was rolling the two heavy bags and she had her carryon with her, a laptop, and the third bag she'd had checked.

He knew she wouldn't like it but he wasn't her father so she didn't need to be angry with him over it. "He said the case he's on means working during the lunch hour. I'm sure he'll join us later to help with the Henry Potter kidnapping."

Her lips parted. "Has my father seen this woman before?"

"Not as far as I know. It was the first time I'd seen her at the agency and she seemed confused about the layout."

"But Dad wasn't working on a case and offered to do it?"

"Yeah." Jason wasn't about to mention the spring in his step when he headed out the door of the office after meeting with her.

"You're sure he hasn't seen her before?"

Jason gave her a sideways glance as he walked her to his vehicle. They finally reached his classy black Jaguar, a yellow stripe running down the middle, making it look like his personal racecar.

He loaded Erin's bags in the trunk while her mouth gaped to see the car he was driving. It had that effect on a lot of people. Which, he had to smugly admit, was the reason he'd driven it to the airport to pick her up. Her dad had said she was going to buy a new car once she got here since hers had been giving her trouble and she sold it, which was why she had flown in, instead of driving home.

"Nice car," she said.

"Too flashy?"

"For doing surveillance, yeah."

He smiled. "This is just my pick up vehicle for she-cats who need a lift."

She raised her brows, wanting to hear more. He didn't say anything further, figuring he'd said too much already.

"As to your question about your dad and his new client and having seen her before, by all appearances, he didn't seem to know her, and vice versa. Anyway, he said we're on our own for lunch, that he knew you'd be starving after the flight, and to grab something to eat before we started delving into this case. I figured we'd make it a working lunch and go over the details while we're eating."

They got into his car, settled against the plush leather seats, and he drove out of the airport to the restaurant. She ran her hand lovingly over the leather.

In that instant, he had the unbidden thought that he wished she was sweeping her hand over his thigh instead. With that in mind, his cock twitched.

"Okay, well we're going to have lunch where *he's* going to have lunch. If it's at the office, we can just order food and have it delivered. If he's gone to someplace else to eat, we can join him there." Erin looked a little peeved.

Jason tried to hide a smile. "What if he is interested in the client and he doesn't want our interference?"

"That's what I want to know." Erin looked out the window. "Teach him to ditch me for another woman."

Now *that* amused Jason. He never thought Erin would be investigating her father's affairs now. He knew if it had been just him, he wouldn't have gone near the restaurant. But he did enjoy the thrill of the hunt.

"Which restaurant?" she asked.

"The Seafood and Steak Alehouse."

"The five-star restaurant?" She shook her head.

"He said he was there on business with the client."

"I bet."

"He's investigating the manager of the restaurant."

"Okay." Erin sounded like she didn't believe there wasn't more to the business of her dad taking the client to the restaurant. "She better foot the bill."

Jason smiled openly that time. "That's what a client normally does."

"Yeah, well we'll see."

"Okay, so what if he is interested in the woman?" Jason figured she'd drop it. Erin might not like that her father was intrigued with another woman, but her own mother and brother had died in a hit-and-run accident when the carjacker had fled from the police after an attempted, failed bank robbery and struck her vehicle ten years ago. That had been a long time ago and Jason felt if her father was ready to move on, Jason was all for it. But he understood Erin's concern that someone might try to replace her mother when her dad was truly devoted to Erin, as much as she was to him.

"Then we investigate her like good PIs do." Erin folded her arms, but then she was looking over his car some more, opening the glovebox, closing it, checking out the visor mirror.

Jason really hadn't expected to be investigating someone Cannon could be seeing. But it was on Erin's head if her dad learned about it and he was angry over it. At least Jason, and he assumed Erin, would attempt to be super spy like in their pursuit of the truth.

"What if they see us at the restaurant?" He could just imagine them being seen and blow their whole case.

"Well, I told you I wanted to go there for lunch, insisted even, so we could discuss our case. I had no idea my dad was going to be there."

He wasn't sure her dad would believe her, and he would know just who put her up to it. "Did you want to do it alone? In case you thought you could be less noticeable than if we both went together."

She eyed him speculatively. "Don't tell me you're afraid of being seen with me and he'll think you had anything to do with this."

"He'll know I told you about his going to the restaurant. He told us to go to the one we usually go to."

"Oh, he did, did he?" She didn't say anything for some time. "Okay, so I was looking up restaurants because I wanted to go to something different this time and found that one. I ate there a long time ago, but I thought it would be fun to go there with you because my dad stood me up. And you didn't tell me he would be there with a client."

Jason shook his head. "He would never believe it. He'll know I told you and he'll know you wanted to go there to check things out with him and the client."

She sighed. "Okay, so we go there because we want to help him with his case and discuss the other one with him."

"He won't believe that either, but at least it sounds more truthful."

"Right. When is he going?"

"Noon, I imagine."

She glanced at the clock in his car. "It's a quarter to twelve. So we'll get there about the same time."

"As long as you don't think your dad will mind. I have a good working relationship with him."

She scoffed. "I have a good father-daughter relationship with him. Though I never expected him not to pick me up at the airport or have lunch with me. It was supposed to be a celebration for me coming home for good."

"I'm sure he'll celebrate with you tonight."

"I'm really not so sure now."

Jason wasn't going to offer to do something with her for tonight. He had his own life to live and entertaining the boss's daughter wasn't something he had planned on.

CHAPTER 3

"*H*ow was the flight?" Jason finally asked Erin on the way to the restaurant. He was just making small talk until they reached the place, though she was looking at her phone now.

"Uneventful, except for the man who wanted more whiskey, and they didn't have enough for him. And the guy who wouldn't turn off his laptop and stow it when we were landing. I was ready to arrest both of them for the fuss they made."

"I can just see you doing it too."

"You betcha."

When Jason and Erin arrived at the restaurant, he parked and belatedly thought about reservations. It was prime time for lunch. He normally ate out around eleven, if he was going to eat at a restaurant because the crowds didn't come that early, normally.

Then they left the car and headed for the restaurant doors. "I didn't see his vehicle in the lot," she said.

"He's probably not here yet. So, since this is an investigation of, I'm not sure what—the manager at the restaurant, the client, or your dad's involvement with the client—what do you suggest we look for?"

"I'd say the manager, if we were going to pull this off, but we don't have any details about the case, so we'll have to wait to hear them from Dad."

"Does that mean lunch is on the agency's account?"

She chuckled. "You're not buying?"

"I figured since we're on a mission, the agency would pick up the tab."

"Yeah, sure."

They entered the restaurant and walked to the hostess stand, the aroma of predominantly seafood and grilled steaks wafting in the air—both of which were a jaguar's kind of meal. "We'd like a seat for two," Erin said.

"Yes." The girl grabbed two menus and Jason was surprised that they had seating for them and didn't have to wait, when others were standing around in large groups waiting for a table. She showed them to a tiny booth for two. As if the two of them were on a date. But it also explained why the booth was available for them.

They took their seats and the hostess handed them their menus. "Your server will be with you shortly."

"Thanks," they both said.

"Do you ever regret leaving the police force and working for my dad?" Erin asked.

"Are you investigating *me* now?"

"No, of course not. It's not a trick question."

"If I'd been a police detective, I would have been doing more investigations and I probably would have liked it better. Arresting people as a police officer and directing traffic wasn't really my thing. Learning the truth about a crime, that was different. I decided to go into the PI field instead. I already had a degree in criminology, and it was great working with your dad. He liked me right off."

"Because he'd been a police detective to begin with."

"Right. And we just hit it off. We work well together. He loves to do anything with the financial aspect of investigations we're doing. I enjoy doing all the criminal investigations for background checks for employment, which can really lead to some interesting cases. Most times agencies who perform that kind of check do more of a superficial investigation. I like to dig deep because I want to make sure the agency is covered in the event a firm hires someone based on our investigation and they turn out not to be who they say they are."

"Does that happen often?"

"No, but when it does, we want to have our bases covered. Your dad likes that I do them because to him, my cases are boring. I feel that way about delving into all the financial details of one of the cases he works. I've had to do it when he's been sick with the flu and I'm happy for him to do them instead. And when he gave me the flu? He got stuck doing background investigations and felt the same way as I did about his jobs."

"And if there's danger involved?"

"We'd let the police—or FBI—handle them, but if it appears that the situation is something we can handle, we certainly will do it."

The server finally brought them glasses of water, a basket of freshly baked loaves of sourdough bread, and butter, and asked them what they would like to order.

Erin chose stuffed mahi-mahi and he ordered salmon.

"They both come with broccoli and baked potatoes," the server said.

"Sounds good," Jason said, Erin agreeing, and he handed the server their menus.

"Would you like anything besides water to drink?"

"Ice tea for me," Erin said.

"Nothing for me." When the server left, Jason asked, "Why did you want to leave the FBI? Your dad said you had a promising career with them." He pulled out his phone and was looking for any information on the news about the missing boy.

Erin was doing the same. "My dad is getting older. I want to spend more time with him. I want to learn the business, the way he does things, and help him out until he wants to retire. Which I don't expect him to do for many years. But I just think it's important to be near to family. My cases were taking me all over the place and I could barely get home for the holidays, much less birthdays or just for visits. While working here, I can just enjoy being with him."

"And if he ends up finding a mate?"

"Then he finds a mate." She tried to sound nonchalant about it, but he didn't think she was really happy about it.

He thought that might change the situation for her here. That she might even wish she hadn't left her job to join her dad at the agency if he was too busy seeing the woman on his time off.

"Listen, I would be glad if my dad enjoyed the company of one of—" She quit speaking when she saw her dad coming into the restaurant with the female client. "Ohmigod, Laura Givens?"

"You know her?"

"Uh, yeah."

"So your dad knew her?"

"Yeah."

"Oh." That sort of soured the milk, Jason thought. But he was also surprised that he hadn't been more aware that they had known each other before. "So in a good way or—"

"She was one of my mom's friends. She was widowed and I think she believed she could slip into Dad's life and take over my mother's role after my mother died."

"Don't tell me. You messed that up for them."

Erin gave him a cutting look. He knew as soon as the words were out of his mouth, he had said the wrong thing.

"Of course not. He did what he wanted to do. I think he felt wary of her motives, and he cut ties with her. Anyway, I haven't seen her in years. I have to admit she looks great." Erin buttered a piece of the bread.

"Maybe he's ready to move on now when he wasn't before. How do you feel about that?"

"She's nice enough. She was always nice to me, but you know how things go. People can be on their best behavior until they get their hooks into the one that they want to have."

Jason laughed. "Sounds like you have trust issues. Or you might be projecting a little."

She scoffed. "I've never been interested in a guy beyond a date or two. They've got supersized egos, are arrogant, carrying around tons of baggage, or self-centered, you name it. I don't intend to be saddled with any prima donna."

He smiled.

"What about you?"

"I haven't been around too many big cats to find one I'd be interested in settling down with. No prima donnas that I've ever met."

"Lucky for you. Did you ever feel you missed out not having your family to raise you?" She sounded serious now, as if she were truly interested and he guessed her father had told her how he had been raised by humans in foster care.

"Yeah. I think that's why I acted out so badly when I was a kid. I needed a jaguar dad—or mom—to knock some sense into me. We're part wild animals, as you well know, and we need someone to set the rules for us the only way that one of our kind can."

"I have to agree with you there. My mother was the one who disciplined me, swatted me with her paw when I did things that could have been dangerous for me."

"And your father indulged you."

"He grew up with two brothers. So yeah, having a little girl in the family made a difference."

"I'm sorry about your twin brother and your mother."

She nodded. "Thank you. It was really hard on both Dad and

me. And I think because of it, he was softer on me. But I still turned out all right."

Jason smiled. "Yeah, even without jaguar parents, I think I did too."

They saw her dad looking around the restaurant, but he was no longer with Laura. Jason realized that he must have smelled their scents. If Cannon and his client had come in first, Jason and Erin could have slipped in unnoticed. Maybe. Unless her dad and Laura had been sitting where they could have seen them. Jason had figured it had been a doomed mission from the first, as far as not getting caught went. And he suspected Erin had known that. But she'd wanted to see who her dad was with no matter what the consequences.

CHAPTER 4

*W*hen Erin's dad finally spied them in their booth at the restaurant, Jason hoped Cannon wouldn't be too peeved with him for bringing Erin here. Here it was the first day, hell, first hour she'd been here, and already she had gotten Jason in trouble.

Cannon was alone so Jason suspected he was coming to speak with them privately. Since Laura knew Erin, Jason suspected that she realized Cannon's daughter was here also. That was the trouble with being able to smell scents so well.

Cannon smiled at them though. Jason had assumed Erin wouldn't get into trouble for it, like Jason would be for letting the cat out of the bag.

"You didn't want to go to the other restaurant?" Cannon asked Erin. "It's your favorite."

She rose from her seat and they hugged. "I love this place and haven't been in years. I figured since I had just gotten in and was starting a new job, I would celebrate before I got to work. I had planned to tell you I wanted to go here. But then Jason was the only one to greet me at the airport and you had a mission for lunch, so I figured I'd go with Jason instead."

"And he told you my mission happened to be here?"

"Yes. I can't tell a lie. It's so packed, I didn't think we'd see you."

Jason sighed.

Her dad smiled at him. "She would have coerced the truth out of you somehow once I didn't pick her up at the airport and stood her up for lunch for her homecoming."

"We thought we could help you with your case, but we also figured you would be working on this other with the Potter boy and wanted to hear what you had to say about it," Erin said.

"Laura hired me for a case concerning the manager, Bristol Donager. He's the one she needs me to investigate. And yes, she knows him and she actually had dated him."

Erin sighed. "You know, Dad, if you're dating her now or are interested in dating her, I'm happy for you."

"Okay, thanks. But it's not my intention. I just planned to work the case for her."

"Whose idea was it for you to have lunch here with her and not just check things out on your own?" Erin didn't seem to buy into his supposed disinterest in Laura.

"Hers."

"So do you need our help?" Jason asked again, because he was ready to work on the Potter case, but if her dad needed help with this one too, he wanted to know of it. Besides, he was ready to get himself out of the boiling stew he felt he had become immersed in and wanted to switch topics.

"No, enjoy your lunch. I'll meet you back at the office later. Sorry I didn't meet you at the airport, Erin. Or have lunch with you. We can have dinner and celebrate your homecoming." Then Cannon gave her another hug and left their table to return to his lunch guest.

"Shoot, I should have asked him if she was picking up his tab," Erin said. "Do you think she's only interested in the case and not in my dad?"

"I believe she's interested in your dad. She could have gone to any PI agency in the city, so who does she choose?"

"My dad because she knows and trusts him."

"Right, but also because he's widowed, a big cat like her. So yeah, I'd say even if she has a case that needs to be investigated privately, she still is interested in your dad."

The server brought their food out and it smelled divinely of spicy salmon, mahi-mahi, broccoli, and buttery potatoes. Jason was glad that Erin had wanted to come here.

"You think that maybe she doesn't really have a case of fraud?" Erin was frowning now as she picked up her knife and fork.

"I'm sure she does have a legitimate case. She probably knows your dad would learn the truth and then he wouldn't be pleased that she's wasted his time. That wouldn't go over well with your dad."

"What if he is the one who made up the case?"

Jason stared at Erin for a moment, chuckled, and then shook his head. "I don't think so, but hell, you know your dad probably better than me."

"Well, I'm hoping that he's not making up stuff, because he most likely would realize I want the best for him."

"Right."

They began digging into their meals.

"This is sure good. I haven't had mahi-mahi in forever, and they really make it right here," she said.

"I agree. I need to come here more often." Jason hadn't thought he'd be enjoying the company also.

"You're invited to dinner whenever we have time to have it," Erin said, as if he should come to the celebratory feast too.

"You probably need some alone time with your dad—"

"Nonsense. We're working together at the office, and it wouldn't hurt to celebrate tonight after work."

"I hadn't expected you to work right after you got here." He admired her for that. He had expected her to spend some time getting settled in.

"I'm excited about it. Since he's doing the financial cases and you're doing background issues, after we resolve the case of the missing boy, I can take all the dangerous ones." She smiled at him and then took another bite of her fish.

"With one of us serving as your backup." He didn't have a problem with taking her with him, being that she was highly trained in the field, but he definitely wasn't letting her do a dangerous mission on her own. That was if they realized it could be dangerous. Some of the most benign situations could turn volatile, depending on who they needed to speak to about a case.

"Of course. I always took precautions when I was on the job and had backup when I went on a hazardous case. I'm not some gung-ho Xena woman."

He smiled at her. She was petite, in good shape, but wasn't muscled like the warrior princess. "Good to know."

"Where do you think we should go with this investigation into the boy's disappearance first?" she asked, glancing at her phone again.

"We talk to all the relatives first. And then his friends." He got a call from a potential client and answered it.

"Hi, I'm Melanie Whitcomb and I need to talk to an investigator about looking for my niece who vanished about three hours ago." Another abduction case?

"Have you called the police?" Even though he was willing to search for another missing child, the police needed to be involved too since they had a lot more resources.

"Yes, but since she's a teen and she's run away from home a number of times, they believe that's probably the case with this. They questioned my sister, Samantha's mother, briefly and her mother's current live-in boyfriend. Samantha has only been missing a short while, but I'm really worried about her. I don't trust the police to take this seriously. I thought a private investigator could look into the situation before any harm comes to her. Not only that, but her cousin is Henry Potter, the boy who is missing also."

"Cousins? Yes, ma'am. We'll be at the office in about half an hour. If you can meet us there, bring a recent picture of Samantha, and tell us all you might know about the case. We'll get started on it right away."

"We? I can only afford one PI."

"We'll only charge you for one, but we have a recent addition to our staff who is a former FBI agent, and she has worked these kinds of cases before. I'll be going with her to make sure she knows all the rules."

Erin raised her brow in response to Jason's comment.

He smiled at her. She'd have to abide by a set of different rules now that she was working as a PI. Though she had gotten her PI license before she came to stay with them so she would be familiar with them.

"Henry's parents hired us to check into his disappearance. It could be they're related," Jason told Melanie.

"Oh, I'm so glad that you have a partner to work with on this and my brother has hired someone to look into Henry's disappearance also. I'll see you soon."

Then Jason told Erin about the case. Her eyes widened. "Omigod, I wonder if Samantha has gone looking for him."

"That's what it could be. For us, this sure was a good day for you to start working at the agency. We can use all the help we can get." Jason finished off his meal and so did she. He wished he could have had a more leisurely lunch with Erin, but a job was a job. He went to pick up the tab, but she did instead.

"The agency will take care of it," she said. "I came here to help my dad with his assignment and conduct business on the other case. He dismissed us, but we still had ordered lunch, so it's on him."

Jason smiled at her, thinking that working with the boss's daughter might just have some perks.

"I love your car, by the way," she said, as they left the restaurant. "I've never seen a Jaguar coupe with a yellow stripe down the hood. It reminds me a little of a jaguar's colors."

"Thanks. They had a black Jaguar with an orange racing stripe that reminded me of a jaguar's colors even more, but I thought the one with the yellow stripe was more striking." It was great for dates. He texted Cannon to tell him that they were on their way back to the office and had a possible teen abduction case in addition to the other one that could be related.

Cannon texted back: *Keep my daughter safe.*

Jason texted: *Will do.*

He figured that Erin might be the one keeping *him* safe. When they reached the office, another car pulled up and they greeted the occupant. She identified herself as the woman who had called them.

But then another car pulled up, and Erin sighed. "Looks like it's getting busy around here."

"Which means it's good you finally showed up." He really hadn't thought he would feel that way. Then they went inside, and Jason motioned to Erin's desk, a nameplate on it already. "That's your desk."

"You are new?" Melanie Whitcomb asked Erin.

"Yes, she just arrived today."

"Good. Maybe her FBI training will help with the case," Melanie said.

Then a man walked into the office and Jason asked, "Can I help you, sir?" He figured Erin could get started on learning about the missing teen and he could see what the man wanted in the meantime.

"Yeah, I need to hire a private investigator to look into my wife's claims that she needs alimony because I'm divorcing her. Yet she hasn't even attempted to get her education, though I've paid for courses several times and she just quits the classes after a while. She's really smart, but she just doesn't want to put in the effort to work on her courses. She uses me as an excuse for not finishing her classes. She did the same thing with work. She'd work at a job and quit it and start another and quit it. She spent every dime I made too."

"I can get a subpoena for her college transcripts through the agency's lawyer. Do you have a lawyer?"

"No, we were trying to do this amicably."

"Okay, well, we'll take care of you."

The guy looked immensely relieved. "Thank you." He signed a contract with Jason, and then the man left.

Jason was about to join Erin and Mrs. Whitcomb, who was dabbing her eyes with a tissue and obviously distraught over this whole business, when he got another call. It was another case of checking out the backgrounds for some more potential employees and he told the personnel manager, "Sure, just fax them over. I'll get on them right away." But he was helping Erin with the two missing kid cases first. When they had a lull in business, he always caught up on his other work when it wasn't as high a priority.

He joined Erin just as Melanie and Erin rose from their seats and she shook Melanie's hand. Jason shook the woman's hand also, and would learn all the details from Erin. As the woman left the agency, he hoped that they could find the girl and the boy quickly.

Erin immediately was texting her father. "I'm letting him know we're headed out the door. I'll give you all the details on the way to Samantha's home. Samantha and Henry Potter are first cousins."

"That sounds like too much of a coincidence to me for the two of them to go missing—if Samantha truly is—for the cases not to be linked."

"I agree." Erin got a text back. "Okay, my dad says that he's on his way back to the office and so he'll manage things from there while we're out of the office. I texted him the information about Melanie's niece's case. He's going to do some online investigating in the meantime into both cases. How did the two of you ever manage without me?"

"Most of the time we were good, but there are times like this when having another investigator can really make a difference. How are you feeling about Samantha's case?"

She explained to him what the woman had told her. "I have to say from what Melanie said about her sister, she's not to be trusted. It's all because of the boyfriends she keeps picking up. Melanie said she has wanted to adopt Samantha because she has three children of her own and all the cousins love getting together. Samantha would have a loving family and Melanie's sister could do whatever she wants as far as it goes with her revolving door of boyfriends. Henry is Melanie's brother's son, and she thinks the two cases are related. She said Samantha and Henry were really close, despite their age difference. She's afraid she's gone out to search for him and will get herself in trouble. As to the boy, Melanie says Henry was just walking to his friend's house and never arrived. I like to keep an open mind about any and every possibility when I work a case like this. You never know what direction it will go in," Erin said.

"That's for sure. I think that's true of just about any case we work, including the more mundane background investigations I do. I found a case where a woman was trying to get employment at a department store and had murdered two people. Her finger-prints were in the system so I got a hit. Now that was a surprise. She got a jail sentence instead of a job. She was so astounded. She said she'd applied and been hired for several jobs and couldn't believe she'd finally been caught up by it. It proves we have to be thorough in our investigations."

"My dad is lucky to have you. You set your standards to reach at a much higher level than some, I'm sure."

"When the news mentioned our agency had helped the police finally catch the woman and send her to Tennessee for trial and ultimately to jail, we ended up getting a ton of background requests for employee applications. I'm sure the other agencies have also beefed up their investigations so we don't leave them behind in the dust."

Erin smiled. "So for dinner tonight, what are you going to grill for us? I want steaks."

He laughed. "I thought your dad was supposed to be the one putting on the feast."

"He'll grill, but you can help him."

"All right. And I'll make some drinks for us."

"That sounds good."

When they finally reached Samantha's home, Erin said, "I didn't expect you to have such a flashy car. Do you do all your surveillance in the Jaguar?"

"No, I have a non-descript car I usually use, but I—"

"Wanted to impress me?"

"Take it for a ride because I don't normally drive it to work."

"You wanted to impress me."

He chuckled. She was astute, he'd give her that, even though he hadn't thought he'd be picking her up from the airport. He'd thought she'd just see it when they got ready to leave the office to go home to their respective residences that night.

CHAPTER 5

"So what do you think about Henry's case? A regular grab and run?" Jason asked Erin.

"He was walking to a friend's house a block away and no one saw anything. You know, the boy has been gone for four hours. I'd say someone enticed him to get in his vehicle, offering some incentive and then just drove off with him."

When Erin and Jason arrived at Samantha's red-brick house, Samantha's mom and her mother's boyfriend wouldn't let them inside to talk. Not that it really mattered. They just wanted to learn what they could and where to take the investigation next.

The mother was at once belligerent. "We already talked to the police because my damn sister stuck her nose in my business. My daughter runs off all the time. And, hell she's only been gone for a couple of hours. The police know it and we know it and there's not a damn thing we can do about it and not enough time has passed to make it an issue anyway."

But what Erin noticed right away was that a female jaguar had been here and that didn't make any sense at all. These people were human.

"She went to Houston," the woman's boyfriend said, surprising Erin and Jason.

The woman looked sharply at him. "Pete…"

Erin wondered if she'd known and it was a secret, or she really hadn't known.

He shrugged. "Samantha was upset about her cousin Henry. She's been calling everyone she knows, calling the neighbors in her cousin's neighborhood, pacing all over the place here. I tried to tell her the police were out in force looking for him, but she was highly agitated and wouldn't settle down. She went over to her uncle's house twice, canvassing the neighborhood. Then she came home again."

Erin thought they might actually make some headway in the case on their first stop.

"The police said she hasn't been gone long enough to raise any red flags. I tried to tell them she's been here and gone looking for her cousin," the boyfriend said. "She and her mom aren't on good terms. But Samantha and I actually talk to each other about her school and dating and books. Anyway, so she left for Houston."

"Why do you think she went to Houston, and did you tell the police that?" Jason asked.

"I did tell them, but they still don't think there is anything to it. She rode with some guy named Dale in a blue, Ford pickup truck, and she went willingly. And she hasn't been gone that long. Her aunt was overly worried about her because of Samantha running away in the past. And with Samantha being so upset over her cousin, her aunt was just really concerned. I don't know Dale's last name. They are in high school together. She goes over to his house to study with him sometimes," Pete said.

"Study, my ass," the mother said.

Everyone glanced at her, but Pete continued, "Anyway, I heard her talking to him on her cell. She said she would meet him outside and he needed to drive her to Houston. Like I said, I told the police, but they didn't believe there was any need for concern. Neither did you," he said to Samantha's mom.

So the mom did know!

"Do you know who Dale is? His last name?" Erin asked the mother, hoping she knew since the boyfriend didn't. And that she'd tell them the truth!

"Dale Baldwin." She scowled at Erin, folding her arms.

"Where were they going in Houston exactly?" Erin asked the woman's boyfriend. "Did she give any clue?"

"No, she just said that they were going to the city."

"Okay, well, thanks so much," Erin told him. They didn't have a whole lot more to go on, but it sounded like Samantha had hitched a ride with a guy she was friends with, and she hadn't been abducted or running away from home. Erin glanced at Jason to see if he had any questions for them, but he was looking at his phone.

"I've got his phone number. Come on." Jason led her back to his car while the door to the house slammed shut. He was on his phone then, entering the number.

"A jaguar's been to the house. Did you smell her?" Erin asked.

"Yeah, I did. I wonder what that's all about. I don't recognize the person's scent, though I don't know all the jaguars in the surrounding areas. She could just be a delivery person and dropped off a package." Jason got an answer to his call. "Hi, I'm Jason Biggerstaff, a private investigator hired by Samantha's aunt, Melanie Whitcomb, to look for Samantha and for her cousin Henry. Samantha's mother's boyfriend said Samantha hitched a ride with you to go to Houston." He and Erin got into his car, and he put the call on Bluetooth. "Are you looking into Henry's disappearance?"

"Yeah, we have a lead."

"Where exactly are you headed? And what makes you think you have a lead for where Henry is?" Jason asked.

"We're driving to the Houston Zoo," Dale said.

"The zoo? Why?" Jason asked.

"The guy who took Henry knows his dad is a zookeeper. He called Samantha to convince her to get Henry's dad's master keys. Now he wants her to bring the keys to the zoo. He said no police or we won't get Henry back. She couldn't tell anyone because she was certain they'd call the police. And she knew I had a truck, so here we are."

"How did she get the keys from her uncle?" Jason asked. "I can't believe her uncle would agree to it and potentially lose his job over it if anyone learned of it. What if this is all a hoax?"

That was Erin's thought also.

"Henry's dad is home sick with the flu. He went home early from work last night and he had his keys at the house," Dale said. "She went to see her uncle, but he was asleep, and she found he'd left the keys on a cabinet in the living room. Her aunt is a nurse and was on duty at the hospital so no one else was at home at the time. Samantha has a key to the front door of their house in case she needed to get away from her mother. Her aunt and uncle didn't want her running off and getting herself into trouble any longer."

"So now Samantha has the keys to the animal exhibits?" Erin asked.

"Yeah, and she has to give them to the man, and he'll release Henry. He said he only needed the keys. He sounded desperate. Samantha had to do it if she wants to help her cousin. She didn't have a choice," Dale said.

"What does the kidnapper plan to do with the keys?" Erin didn't like the sound of it. He could release a bunch of the animals from their cages. She'd heard of a jaguar escaping his habitat enclosure and killing eight animals at a zoo. What if while the zoo was open, like now, the kidnapper released some predators on the unsuspecting crowds. They sure didn't want that to happen. And if the boy was there, Samantha and Dale too, they could be injured or killed if the man did that. Not to mention she worried he might try to take Samantha and Dale hostage too.

"He wouldn't say. He just said no police involvement, or we'd never see Henry again. Even I like the kid," Dale said. "And I don't want to see him get hurt."

"Can we speak to Samantha?" Erin asked, wanting to make sure she was with him, unharmed, and she wasn't being coerced to go with Dale. Not that she thought Samantha was, but she had to make sure. "I'm Erin Chambers, by the way, a private investigator, but also former FBI and I've handled cases like this before."

"Yeah, this is Samantha." Her voice was breaking, and Erin wanted to give her a hug and rescue her cousin for her. "I'm all right. I can never tell my mother anything. Pete, her boyfriend, is easier to talk to than her. We didn't tell him where we were going because we knew Pete would call the police and not let us put ourselves at risk. Pete must have overhead me talking to Dale about going to the city. I didn't mention where in Houston we were going. Promise me you won't tell the police."

"No, we won't," Erin said. "We're on your side. We'll help you out any way that we can. We're on our way there to meet up with you. What about Dale? Does the kidnapper know he's with you?"

"Yeah. I had to tell him because I didn't have any way of getting to the zoo. The man sounds desperate. I'm really worried. What if he gets upset about you being there and thinks you're the police? He might run off with Henry or hurt him," Samantha said.

"We'll be acting like we're a couple just enjoying a visit to the zoo. We'll be watching you but stay far enough away from you so as not to spook him. He won't know we're with you. I've done all kinds of cases like this," Erin said.

"All right, but don't screw it up," Samantha said, her voice angry through her tears.

Erin sure hoped that they weren't making a mistake by not turning this over to the police. She couldn't believe she'd get involved in a PI case that was so much like handling one of her FBI cases, except without the backup.

"Okay, we're parking at the zoo right now. How long will it take you to get here?" Dale asked.

"Another ten minutes. Sit tight and we'll follow you in," Jason said.

"All right." Dale sounded relieved they would have someone there to help them out in case they got themselves into real trouble.

"I didn't want to steal my uncle's keys." Samantha was sniffling and sounding like she was barely able to stop from crying.

"We'll save your cousin, Samantha. We'll free him." Erin prayed they would without any harm coming to any of the kids. She could just imagine the case being on the news, and her buddies in the FBI seeing her involved in the whole mess. But hopefully they would manage this, make a citizen's arrest, free the kids, rescue the zoo keys, and all without causing any trouble.

"Okay, we're here," she said. "We're parking now. We'll meet you at the ticket counter. Well, we'll follow you in from a distance."

"What are you driving?" Dale asked.

"A black Jaguar with a yellow stripe," Jason said.

"Oh, hot damn. I see it," Dale said. "I mean, how could anyone not see it. If we weren't supposed to be sneaking around the place, I'd come over and look at it. We see you now getting out of the car. Both of you are wearing black—she's in black leather and you're in a black turtleneck and a black leather jacket."

"Yeah," Jason said. "We'll make sure that we're a few people behind you at the ticket booth."

"All right."

Then, to Erin's surprise, Jason grabbed her hand, turned her, and pulled her against his body hard—and he *was* hard, sculpted muscle pressed hot against her body—and kissed her mouth. His lips were sizzling against her chilled ones, and she couldn't help that her eyes widened, while his, she swore, were smiling. He was a great kisser; she just hadn't expected it in a million years.

"What was that for?" she asked, easing away, trying not to sound shocked or annoyed with him. He was one charmer, even if he wasn't trying to be.

"We're supposed to be a couple. If the kidnapper sees us here without kids and that were just visiting the zoo as a couple, he might be suspicious. He won't believe we're two cops if we look like we're dating or married," Jason said, taking her hand and leading her to the ticket booth.

Even holding her hand like this felt way more intimate than she thought it could. Never had she thought she'd be holding the sexy cat's hand on a walk through the zoo on a kidnapping case, or that she would even see him as sexy! "If he saw what you drove up in, he won't either." She could imagine the kidnapper admiring the Jaguar, like everyone else did and not paying a whole lot of attention to the couple arriving in it.

Jason smiled. "Yeah, you're right about that."

They finally reached the ticket booth line and were located about three families behind Dale and Samantha. They recognized Samantha from the photo her aunt had given to Jason—a black-haired girl, wearing jeans, sneakers, and a blue jacket. The boy was wearing jeans, black sneakers, and a dark gray hoodie, his hood up. Both teens fidgeted as they got their tickets and moved slowly into the zoo, looking around for Henry and the man who had taken him, most likely. Samantha's phone jingled and she answered it.

Was it the kidnapper calling?

Samantha said, "Okay. We didn't call the police." She started crying and Dale rubbed her back and took the phone from her. Erin was glad Dale was there for Samantha. She wouldn't have managed on her own, Erin figured.

"We're headed to the big cats' exhibit," Dale said. "Don't hurt Henry."

With the jaguar's hearing, Erin and Jason were able to make out what Samantha and Dale said to the man.

Erin was going to pay for the tickets, though it didn't matter as they would charge them to the agency account, but Jason got them and leaned over and kissed her, then slipped his credit card into his wallet.

Okay, more of the show, as if he were taking her on a date. "Do you want to get me a cookie?" She figured she might as well play along and see if he was game.

He laughed.

"I'm serious."

"Yeah, I know. That's why I laughed. Sure. I'll get you a cookie. You ate all your lunch."

That had her chuckling. Maybe he wasn't so bad after all. Before, when she'd visited her dad at the agency, Jason had been aloof, and they had seemed to argue about everything. She'd had the distinct impression that he didn't like the idea she would return someday to take over the business and he would be working for her. Maybe she was wrong. Maybe they could work together successfully. So far, things were going well between them on the case.

"Do you know what you want?" Jason asked.

"Chocolate chip." She imagined if the kidnapper saw her and Jason and she was eating a cookie at the zoo, it really would look like they were here just to have fun.

"Okay, you watch the kids and I'll grab your cookie for you."

She observed the kids as they roamed through the zoo, stopping to look in the tiger exhibit while Dale was on Samantha's phone still, not talking, just listening to instructions, Erin figured.

Then Jason came out of the shop with a bag and handed it to her. She pulled out a chocolate chip cookie and peered at the other cookie inside and smelled her delightful chocolate one and the other was a cinnamon and sugar-coated cookie. "A snicker-doodle cookie."

"Yeah, mine. You didn't think I could pass up having dessert too while you were eating in front of me, did you?"

Smiling, she really hadn't thought he'd get one too. "Okay, let's go. They're at the tiger exhibit but now they're on the move again."

"All right." He pulled out his cookie and ditched the paper sack in a trash receptacle. He took a bite, his hand on hers as they headed toward the tiger exhibit. "This is good." He smiled down at her and kissed her forehead. "You have a melted chocolate chip on your lip." But he didn't wait for her to lick it off and did the honor himself instead.

Now that enticed her to want to pull him into her arms and kiss him. "Were you ever undercover when you were on the police force?" she asked.

"Nah, not me."

"Well, you do a good job at it."

"Thanks. They're headed for the snow leopard exhibit."

"You sure know where everything is," she said, surprised he had come to the zoo before.

"Yeah, I bring all my dates here."

She glanced up at him, not believing him.

He chuckled. "My sister, Layla Whitson, has two kids, a boy and a girl, Ethan and Kristie, twins, six years old. Whenever I have some free time, I go with her and the kids to the zoo."

"Aww. I didn't know you had a sister." And Erin sure had him pegged wrong.

"Yeah, she was in foster care like me, and we had lost touch. I just finally found her, and she and the kids love trips to the zoo. She's an insurance adjuster and puts the kids in a jaguar daycare, though they have wolves in it too now."

"Oh, how cool. And this cookie really hit the spot. Thanks." She finished off her cookie and then pulled out her phone to text her dad with an update. Then she pocketed her phone and saw a man standing with Henry. "Right up there. There's a man dressed in blue denim, jacket, black boots, blond, wearing an olive drab backpack and he's got the boy with him. The boy appears to be really happy, smiling, not upset though."

"Yeah, I agree. Samantha and Dale are approaching him," Jason said. "Do you smell that same female jaguar's scent around here? I keep getting hints of it."

"Yes, I'm smelling it too. The wind's whipping around so much, it's hard to catch where it's coming from."

They quickened their pace while the man was watching the teens and nothing else.

Samantha handed the man the keys and he released the boy. The kidnapper hurried off past the location of the snow leopard exhibit.

Erin and Jason reached the location of the kids and made sure Henry was okay, but immediately, Erin smelled the scent of a wolf on the boy, and the boy himself was a jaguar shifter. She looked sharply at Jason, his gaze colliding with hers. The kidnapper was a wolf? But they also had found the owner of the female jaguar scent—Samantha.

"Can we call 911 now?" Dale asked.

No! They couldn't allow the man to be taken into custody. Not when he was a fellow shifter.

"No!" Samantha said, smelling that Erin and Jason were jaguars too and she had to know the man holding her cousin hostage had been a wolf. It would be disastrous for them to call the police on the man.

"No, we'll call the police. The three of you—" Jason said.

"I'll go after the kidnapper." Erin needed one of them to stick with the kids. "You stay with the kids. Then we can sort this out." She couldn't believe the man who had taken the boy hostage to get the zoo keys was a wolf! And that Henry and Samantha were jaguars. Dale was the only one who wasn't a shifter.

"You're going to let a woman go after a dangerous kidnapper while you stay with us?" Dale asked, sounding like he was in disbelief.

"I'm a former FBI agent." Erin tried not to sound annoyed that the boy would think she couldn't handle this.

"He was nice to me," Henry said. "Don't hurt him. While we were waiting, he got me this cool dinosaur hat, pizza, rode with me on the carousel three times, even got me popcorn and food to feed to the giraffes."

"You stay with the kids. I'm calling Everett and Demetria Anderson to help out," Jason said, without discussing it further with her and tore off.

She knew Everett and Demetria were jaguars with the United Shifter Force that dealt with problem shifters, but, yeah, that's what Erin figured. Working with Jason meant she'd have to go by *his* rules. *Not happening.*

CHAPTER 6

*J*ason knew from the irked expression Erin wore that she was really pissed off at him for going after the kidnapper and leaving her with the kids. Maybe she didn't like kids. What did he know?

Now he wondered what the deal was with Henry and Samantha. Had they been adopted? Or were they foster kids like he'd been?

Either he or Erin had to "protect" the kids, *rather* in truth, protect the wolf shifter from being arrested by the police, yet still ensure the kids didn't call the police and felt like they were being protected by someone who knew what she was doing. Jason assumed Erin would know how to reassure the kids better—especially Samantha because they were both big she-cats—than he would. This was a case of needing help from the jaguar police force and he called a friend of his, Everett Anderson, who worked for the jaguar-run United Shifter Force to help them out.

"Hey, Everett, this is Jason Biggerstaff. I have a real problem. I'm chasing down a wolf shifter who is at the Houston Zoo, carrying a set of keys to the zoo enclosures, and I'm afraid he's going to try and release a jaguar, thinking he's a shifter, maybe? There are no wolves at the zoo. He has already been involved in the kidnapping of Henry Potter, who turned out to be one of our kind. So is his first cousin, Samantha. My new partner"—she really wasn't Jason's partner, and she probably would want to strangle him after he left her with the kids—"and I are here. You might know Erin Chambers—"

"FBI agent. Yes. She's been in the news."

"Right. She's joined her father's agency and she's staying with the kids so that they don't call the authorities on this one. Samantha was just trying to reach her cousin to rescue him, but she and Henry are jaguars; Samantha's boyfriend isn't a shifter."

Vehicle doors were slamming, and Jason heard Everett's SUV tear off. He figured Everett was on his way.

"My mate is coming with me. Demetria and I will take the shifter into custody, so that the kids will know that the situation has been taken care of. We'll have to see what to do about the cousins, if none of the parents are shifters."

"They aren't."

"The kids need their own kind to befriend them and help them deal with the issue of being shifters like us, if they don't have help with it already."

"Agreed." Jason followed the kidnapper as he looped his way around to the snow leopard exhibit, not the jaguar enclosure where he thought the man would go and he stopped. What was going on? Had he seen Jason following him? "He's at the snow leopard's exhibit. I'm going to stop him now."

"Be careful."

"Yeah." Jason pocketed his phone, though he still had it open so Everett and Demetria could listen in on what was going on and hurried to intercept the man at the zoo employee's door to the enclosure. As soon as the kidnapper found the correct key, Jason reached him and grabbed his arm to stop him from opening the door. "You're one of us. A wolf shifter though, right? What the hell is wrong with you? Kidnapping a kid? Trying to get into an exhibit to what? Release a predator? Are you crazy?"

"I'm an Arctic wolf shifter. A *lupus garou*. William is a shifter also. We've got to get him out of there."

"A snow leopard?"

"Yeah, he's a friend, okay?"

"Who are you?"

"Brian Jenkins. I didn't know who to contact to help me here. I was at the zoo, smelled that the boy was a jaguar shifter, and his father is a zookeeper. If his dad had been a jaguar shifter, I would have told him what was going on. But he's human. Henry was too scared to get the keys from his dad's house, so he said his cousin Samantha would. She's older and is a jaguar shifter too, he told me. I wanted to leave Henry behind, but he begged me to take him with me to see the snow leopard. And he said it was the only way for us to get Samantha to bring us the keys."

"You're telling me the kid planned this?"

"Yeah, so we could free the snow leopard."

"I take it you're not from here." Jason assumed Brian would know about the jaguar shifters in the area, maybe the jaguar policing force, and could have asked for help. This was not the way to go about it.

"We're from Alaska."

"Alaska?"

"Yeah. I'm sorry. I had to get William out of there."

"We're at the zoo," Everett said. "Are you still at the snow leopard exhibit?"

"Yes." Then Jason explained to Brian who was coming. "They're with a jaguar/wolf policing force. We have to get you out of here before the police arrest you for kidnapping a kid."

"The boy went willingly with me. He's a jaguar shifter. I promised him I'd show him a snow leopard shifter. But they have

William locked up in quarantine inside. I've been following any leads I could to try and get him out of there. His two triplet brothers are coming in today to help me, but I couldn't wait. Not when I thought I had a surefire way to release him."

"This isn't the way to do it."

"I didn't know what else to do. I was afraid his brothers would do something even more drastic."

Jason shook his head. "This is about as drastic as they come."

"Let me unlock the door and give him his clothes at least. He can shift, dress, and come out with us," Brian said.

"I see you," Everett said, he and his mate, Demetria, headed their way.

"Good. Now what do we do?" If Jason had had training in matters like this, he would know what the protocol was, but he didn't.

* * *

ERIN HAD WAITED LONG ENOUGH, getting a quick text from Jason telling her they had the situation in hand. *Just take care of the kids and we'll deal with this.*

Everything was under control? This was a virtual disaster.

Jason texted: *Feed the kids. Keep them happy.*

She couldn't believe it!

She texted her dad with an update: *Dad, Jason is working on the situation with a wolf shifter who took the boy hostage. Jaguar shifters are coming to Jason's aid. And Henry and his cousin Samantha are shifters too.*

Her dad texted back: *What are you doing?*

She texted: *Babysitting.*

Her dad didn't respond, and she figured he probably assumed she wasn't happy with the arrangement.

"Okay, who all else wants pizza? I know Henry had some

already, but if you'd like something else, we can go get it," Erin said to the kids.

"Aren't we going to report the kidnapping?" Dale asked.

"Jason has reinforcements that just arrived and they're taking care of it. He told me to take you all to get something to eat or see at the zoo, whatever you'd like, until we resolve this."

"What about Henry's family?" Samantha asked, holding her cousin's hand.

"We're notifying them." In due time.

"I gotta pee," Henry said.

Erin didn't want him to go alone into the bathroom after what had happened to him already. Dale seemed to feel the same way. "Me too. Let's go."

Perfect. Now Erin could talk to Samantha alone.

"Were you and Henry adopted? Foster kids?" Erin quickly asked.

Samantha shook her head. "I was bitten. A couple of years ago, I went to a party that everyone was going to at one of the kid's homes when their parents were gone on a weekend trip. I was looking for a bathroom and the downstairs one was occupied. So I went upstairs and opened a door, thinking maybe it was another bathroom, but it was a bedroom. I don't know even what happened exactly. I mean, in a flash there was a leopard leaping at me."

"A jaguar."

"Yeah. I didn't know what the difference was at the time. I just thought it was a leopard. It bit me and then I stumbled out of the room, and it slammed the door shut. I'd had too much to drink and from the shock from getting bitten, I don't know. I just remembered waking up on the floor in the hallway, the bite on my arm was gone, and I figured someone had put something in the punch and I had just"—she shrugged—"had been hallucinating and passed out."

"Then later you shifted?"

"Yeah. I was home the first time, and my mom was ragging on me about going to the party without permission—I don't know how she always learns about these things—and I had to race to my room and lock the door. I just felt like I was burning up, feverish, but then I somehow knew I had to take off my clothes. Maybe because of the heat I was feeling. The next thing I knew, I was a jaguar, and I was afraid I was having flashbacks about seeing a leopard, well, jaguar. I just couldn't believe it."

"When did this happen?" Erin asked.

"When I was fifteen. So I've had this condition for two years. I can control it now. I couldn't always in the very beginning. I had to skip a lot of school." She looked askance at Erin. "What's your story?"

"I was born a shifter. And we have lots of people who will love to meet you."

"That...that man...he was like us, but not? The one who took Henry hostage?"

"Yeah. I think he's a wolf shifter and got some idea a shifter is locked up in an enclosure. Others are here to try and help him."

"We can't call the police, can we?"

"No. We can't put this on TikTok or Instagram or any of the other social media sites. The police, FBI could get involved and we'd be in trouble."

"I want to help the man who's locked up. If one of us were—"

"The others will do it." At least Erin hoped they would. Though she also wished she was there with them, trying to figure out how to do this. Then again, Samantha needed her too and she was glad they had this talk. "And your cousin?"

Samantha chewed on her bottom lip. "That was all my fault. I was babysitting him, and he kept doing things I told him not to because he wanted my attention. I was on my phone. Anyway, I told him if he didn't tell anyone, I'd show him something really cool."

"You shifted."

"Yeah, I came out of the bedroom as a jaguar and he tripped on a toy, trying to get away from me. He fell and hit his head and was bleeding. I licked him, not thinking it would do anything to him. I just wanted him to know I wasn't going to hurt him. Within the hour, he was yanking off his clothes and I realized the mistake I'd made. He shifted into a jaguar. The only good thing that came of it was that his head healed much faster. Of course, he thinks it's the coolest thing ever, but I'm worried he'll tell someone what we are, bragging, or even bite someone like the guy did to me."

Henry and Dale came out of the restroom and Dale said, "Hey, does the offer of pizza still stand?"

"Yeah, come on," Erin said, and she rubbed Samantha's back, telling her that she had a new friend who would be there for her anytime she needed her to. She was also thinking that if she and her mother didn't get along at all, and Samantha wanted to join a jaguar family, she'd do what she could to find one for her. As to Henry? They needed to take care of that situation too.

JASON COULDN'T BELIEVE he was in the middle of a jaguar forces action to help rescue a shifter, and he was hoping that Erin was doing fine with the kids.

"Okay, go ahead, unlock the door," Everett said. "We'll watch out for anyone else who might approach the enclosure."

Then Brian went inside, and Jason was hoping the hell he was right about the snow leopard being a shifter or he could be in harm's way. The next thing they knew, Brian and a black-haired man pulling on a jacket, hurried out of the zookeeper's entry to the exhibit and they locked the door. They hurried away from the door. They needed to get the keys back to Samantha's uncle, and they needed to get Brian away from here too. And deal with the issue of the boy being taken.

Jason called Erin right away. "We've got Brian and the man he was trying to rescue. William Wright is a snow leopard."

"Really? Wow. You'll have to tell me how that all came about. We're at the café having pizza."

"I'll tell everyone. We'll meet you there and we'll get Henry home."

"What about Dale and Samantha?"

"Dale can drive Samantha to Henry's home, and we'll give her all kinds of resources that she can have so we can connect her and Henry with our kind."

"Okay. We've talked, but we need more time together to talk about all this."

"All right. That sounds like a good idea. I hope you're not too irritated with me over taking care of this and leaving you behind to take care of the kids."

"We had a good talk. But next time—"

He smiled. "Hopefully we won't have another time like this. Okay, we're nearly there. By the way, did you see the weather report?"

"No, what's up?"

"Bitterly cold weather coming. Snow. Ice. Freezing."

"Here?"

"Yeah, so I hope you brought some warm clothes with you. It's bound to turn into an Ice Age."

Then they reached the café and headed inside. Erin smiled at Jason as if she were seeing her rescuer come to save her. He smiled back; glad she wasn't angry with him leaving her with the kids. She also waved at Demetria and Everett.

"Hey." Demetria gave Samantha and Henry a broad smile. "We're so glad we could assist you."

"He's the kidnapper," Dale said, his mouth gaping.

"He isn't. I mean, he just desperately needed our help, and we are so grateful to you, Samantha and Henry, for coming to our aid." Everett showed his badge and so did Demetria.

"Agent Daniels was undercover," Demetria said.

Henry's eyes were huge. "I told you he was really nice to me. Did I help you with it too?"

"You sure did." Brian smiled. "Thanks for helping me."

Dale shook his head. "This was an undercover operation? With a kid?"

"Yeah, sorry, Dale. That's why we couldn't call the police. They would have botched everything," Samantha said, as if she'd been in on this the whole time.

"Okay." Dale scratched his head. "I don't understand what Henry was needed for though."

"That part of the assignment is strictly confidential," Everett said.

"Did you get enough to eat?" Erin asked the kids.

"Yeah, thanks," Samantha said.

"Can you do one more thing for us?" Demetria asked Samantha. She handed her the set of keys to the zoo.

"Yeah, sure. I will," Samantha said.

"How are you going to get in without being seen this time?" Dale asked.

"I'm going to say my mom and I had a fight, and I went over to make my uncle some chicken soup if he's feeling better. And I'll leave the keys where I found them," Samantha said. "My aunt will still be at the hospital working."

"And your mom? Are you going to tell her where you are?" Erin asked. "She thinks you've run away."

"I'm going to tell Pete. But I need to see if I can live somewhere else." Samantha sounded like her mind was made up.

"We can make that happen," Demetria said.

Jason was glad for that if it was really something Samantha wanted to do.

"What about Henry?" Samantha asked.

"We'll have to discuss this with you and him later," Demetria said.

Then Samantha called Pete to tell him she was on the way to her uncle's place and was fine. She was just with her friend Dale and Henry was fine too and on his way home. Jason called Henry's family and told them the boy was with agents and would be home soon. That he was perfectly all right.

After that, they headed for the parking lot for their cars, but Dale had to look over Jason's sporty Jaguar first and he let Dale, Samantha, and Henry sit in it, which they loved.

"Okay, well, we'll follow you out of here," Jason said to Dale.

"You'll ride with us," Demetria said to Henry "We'll be taking you to your home, and Jason and Erin will follow us there because they found you with their investigative expertise." Demetria smiled. "And, Samantha, you need to come too so you can slip the keys back to where they belong."

"The two of you have to come with us also," Everett said to Brian and William.

Samantha hugged Erin and then Demetria. "Thank you." Then she got into the car with Dale and the others loaded up in their vehicles and headed out.

"I hope this doesn't come back to bite us," Erin said to Jason.

"Yeah, I know. Demetria and Everett are going to talk to Henry about what went down. Henry's parents aren't jaguars though."

"We'll have to do something about Henry too. Since he's young, I don't think he'll want to leave his family, unlike Samantha does. There wasn't any indication he's unhappy with his homelife," Erin said.

"Henry's parents might need to be turned," Jason said.

"And the person who turned Samantha?" Erin asked.

Jason shook his head. "We might never know the truth about that."

Erin explained to Jason all that Samantha had told her then.

"Hopefully Samantha can sneak the keys back into her uncle's house without letting on about it when we all end up at the Potters' home," Jason said.

"I just hope we can all keep our stories straight. Especially the kids," Erin said.

Amen to that.

CHAPTER 7

On the way to Henry's home, Demetria called Jason and Erin on Bluetooth to discuss the situation with Henry and his parents.

"Okay, we can only think of one way to handle this. Samantha wants to live with a jaguar family. Finding one for her won't be a problem. We've talked to Henry about his relationship with his parents and he loves them. He wants us to turn them so they can be one big, happy jaguar family," Demetria said. "And Samantha, if she wants, can live with them too."

"Would Henry's parents agree to that? Her other aunt, Melanie, said she could stay with her and her family, but I don't believe we should turn her aunt and her aunt's family," Erin said.

"No, we agree," Everett said. "Normally, we wouldn't even consider doing something like this to Henry's parents, but he's young, we don't have shifting issues like the wolves do with the moon phases and all, and hopefully we can do this so that Henry can grow up with his own family like he should. Except they'll be changed. And Henry can join the group of homeschooled jaguars so that he doesn't get himself into trouble with other kids. Samantha seems to be fine in that regard. But Henry is at the age where he might feel he has to prove himself and we don't want him to show off his jaguar abilities."

That was one thing as PIs, Jason and the other investigators in their agency didn't need to concern themselves with turning humans—normally. All they had to do was call on the jaguar agency to deal with it. He never thought they would turn parents though because a child had been turned. Not that the idea didn't have merit, but he'd just never considered having to do it.

When they ended the call, Erin let out her breath. "That's something I'd never have to do as an FBI agent."

"Not as a private investigator either. And I'm glad for that." Jason glanced at Erin, not sure how she felt about any of this. "We need to be there to corroborate what had happened, but we can wait until Demetria and Everett turn the parents. Then speak to them also."

"No way. We need to help out if the parents totally freak out. Which they might."

When Everett and Demetria pulled into the driveway of Henry's home, Jason and Erin parked behind him. The wolf shifter and snow leopard pulled up and parked and Dale drove up in his truck right after that. Samantha got out and joined the others, waving goodbye to Dale and he drove off.

Then they all went to the door with Henry. When the dad answered the door, he looked pale, probably from being sick with the flu, but he brightened upon seeing Henry, hugging him. "God, I'm so glad you're all right. What, where—"

Everett and Demetria showed him their badges. "Can we go inside and talk?" Everett asked.

"Yeah, sure. If you're not afraid of getting sick from the flu."

As jaguar shifters with faster healing genetics, they knew it would take care of it quickly if any of them got it.

Samantha gave her uncle a hug. "How are you feeling?"

"Awful, but so much better now just seeing Henry and knowing he's safe and home."

Mr. Potter had everyone move to the living room, but Samantha said, "I need to use the bathroom. I'll be right back." She slipped away and Jason figured she was putting the zoo keys back where they belonged.

"I've called my wife. She's a nurse at the hospital and she's on her way home," Mr. Potter said.

"Okay, good," Everett said.

Henry was cuddled next to his dad on one of the couches and Jason and the others could see they were close.

"I know who you are," Mr. Potter said to Jason. "The PI we hired. And the special agents have identified themselves. Who is everyone else?"

"I'm working with the PI agency also. My dad runs it," Erin said.

"The other men have statements to make once your wife gets here," Everett said.

"Witnesses?"

"From Alaska, yes," Demetria said.

Then Jason heard a car arrive and a car door open and slam shut. Within minutes, Mrs. Potter barged into the house. Henry jumped up from the couch and rushed across the floor to hug his mom. She was crying and hugging him to pieces. He started crying too.

Jason didn't want to turn these people. But he didn't think they had a whole lot of choice. Not if they wanted to protect Henry. They seemed to be a perfectly happy family and separating them wasn't an option.

Everett explained who they all were and then Demetria asked if she could use the bathroom.

Jason figured it was going to go down now, before they explained what had actually happened to Henry and to Samantha also. Then Everett gave up the floor to Jason and Erin since they were working the case and had learned where the kids had been.

"I'm going to check on Demetria," Everett said, and left the room.

"We learned from Samantha's mother's boyfriend, Pete, that Samantha had gone with her boyfriend to Houston and once we contacted Dale, we learned they were headed to the zoo," Jason said, trying not to glance back at the hallway leading to where both Everett and Demetria had disappeared.

"The zoo?" Mrs. Potter said, looking astonished.

That's when two jaguars rushed into the living room. There was no sense in them coming in quietly because they couldn't have approached the couple without terrifying them no matter how they did it. They leaped over the couch and Mrs. Potter threw her arms up in self-defense, her husband trying to protect Henry and his wife.

Demetria bit the wife on the arm, gently though. As powerful as a jaguar's bite was, they could crush a tortoise's shell, so they had to be careful. Everett bit Mr. Potter and then the two jaguars raced off, jumping over the furniture and back down the hall.

The Potters were gasping for air, terrified, expecting the big cats to return at any moment.

"We're all jaguar shifters," Samantha explained.

"Me too." Henry hugged his mom and Samantha hugged her too and then her uncle.

"Well, I'm a snow leopard," William said.

"And I'm an Arctic wolf," Brian said.

Samantha left the room and returned with a first aid kit and then Jason and Erin began taking care of the Potters' bite wounds. "The bites will heal up in no time," Jason said.

And then everyone began telling their story while Everett and Demetria returned to the living room as if nothing strange had happened.

Of course Henry's parents didn't believe any of this was real. How could it be? But the shifters hadn't wanted to embarrass them by stripping in front of them and then shifting. Even Samantha and Henry could have been uncomfortable with it.

"Can we see what you look like?" Henry asked Brian and William. "You promised."

"Yeah, sure," Brian said, glancing at the Potters to make sure that they were all right with it.

They just looked shocked. Finally, the dad said, "Yeah, sure, go for it."

Jason was looking forward to seeing the snow leopard especially since he hadn't seen a shifter like that before. He suspected the others felt the same way. He didn't know of anyone who had even known they existed.

Brian and William left the living room and in the hall out of sight of the Potters, they stripped and shifted and then they ran into the living room and everyone was surprised to see them— especially the snow leopard.

William was beautiful and fluffy, and he reminded Jason that Brian said he had two brothers that were coming to his aid, and he hoped Brian, or William, had informed them already that they were fine. Brian, likewise, was a beautiful white, fluffy wolf.

Henry and Samantha had to pet the snow leopard and wolf, though the Potters looked horrified that they might bite them. Then Brian and William left the living room to shift and dress.

"I can shift for you," Henry said to his parents then. "I know you don't believe it." Unabashedly, and probably thrilled he could finally tell his parents about it and show them he was really a shifter, he yanked off his clothes, his mother objecting. But then the boy was naked and at once he was shifting, a blur of forms between a human and a jaguar cub so fast, if anyone had blinked, they wouldn't have seen it. His parents' mouths gaped in astonishment.

But he was adorable and much less scary as a cub.

"You can hug him, pet him, love on him," Samantha said. "He's your son, and perfectly safe to be around. We just needed you to be the same as us so it would be safe for Henry."

"And we have families who homeschool the kids so Henry would do well to join them. Speaking of which, we'll have to get you together with others of our kind. We're not like a wolf pack —" Demetria said.

"Like we are—well, back home," Brian said, returning to the living room, fully dressed and William joined them after a few more minutes.

"Erin and I can shift for you also," Jason said.

"Yeah, I'd love to see you too," Samantha said. "Seeing each other helps us to recognize each other later. Though this is the first time I've seen any jaguars other than my cousin and the one who bit me and turned me. So this is a real treat for me."

Erin glanced at Jason, and he wondered if she hadn't wanted to shift at the house. He guessed he should have asked her first. Still, after he got up from the other couch and headed to the hallway, she went with him.

She raised her brows at him. He began stripping and smiled. "Sorry, I shouldn't have volunteered you."

"No big deal. I just thought that might have been a little much for them to see all of us shift." She eyed him as she began stripping out of his clothes. He couldn't help watching her removing her clothes either. He realized he was super interested in seeing Erin naked, that he wanted to see more of her, and he attributed his change of heart to the fact that she was now living here, and he wanted to get to know her better.

Then they shifted and instead of just running down the hall, he rubbed against her, and she rubbed against him as big cats would, their sensitive whiskers touching each other's. And then they loped into the living room as if they were just two more shifter models coming down the runway, showing off their fur coats.

Henry was curled up against his mom's lap now and she was

stroking him, and Jason was glad she was getting more comfortable with the notion.

"Okay, there's another matter we want to discuss," Demetria said, "Samantha wants to live with a jaguar shifter family. We have several jaguar families who would be willing to take her in. We know her Aunt Melanie wanted to, but she and her family aren't shifters. Would you be willing to take her in instead?"

Samantha said, "Yes, that works for me!" She gave her uncle and aunt a hug and then left the living room. "Be right back. I have to show off my jaguar coat too."

Erin and Jason returned to the hallway once Samantha had shifted, and she rubbed against them in a big cat greeting. Jason was glad she instinctually knew to do that.

Then they shifted and began getting dressed. "Well, this has been quite a day," Erin said to Jason.

"Yeah, guess you're about ready for our celebration dinner tonight."

"You bet."

Then Henry's mom said, "Yes, we'll take Samantha in. She's always been so good with Henry. And we love her like she is our own daughter. Was it because she'd turned him? No. She was always offering to babysit him."

Samantha purred, and then rubbed up against both her aunt and uncle. Henry wasn't shifting back as if he was so happy he could do this in front of his parents and not hide the fact any longer that he was going to just stay like that.

But then the dad frowned. "I'm burning up with fever."

"It's the shift coming on," Erin said as she and Jason were fully dressed and joined them.

"I thought it was the effects of the flu." Mr. Potter rushed out of the room.

Jason figured they would all hang around until the Potters had both shifted so they could actually feel the change and then discuss anything further they needed to with them.

William got a call on his phone and said, "My brothers are getting into the airport. If you all don't need to arrest us or anything—we need to go pick them up."

"We'll have a celebration at Strom Hart's mansion tomorrow night," Everett said. "He's a jaguar shifter who is hosting the event, and I'm sure everyone would be thrilled to see the snow leopards. That includes the Potter family too. We'll pick you up and take you there."

Once it was agreed upon, William and Brian left. Mr. Potter came into the living room as one big jaguar, and then his wife had to leave to shift.

Jason was going to contact Cannon and tell him they accomplished two of their cases, but noticed Erin was texting him instead. He rubbed her back and she glanced up at him. He smiled.

Demetria and Everett said they were hanging around after that as this was more their kind of work and they wanted to help the family adjust to their new jaguar senses. Then Jason and Erin left to return to the office to see what else they had to deal with, though it was about dinner time and time to finally celebrate Erin's homecoming.

CHAPTER 8

*W*hen they arrived at the agency, Erin's father was on the phone and waved for Erin to come in. Her dad rose from his chair and gave her a hug, then ended the call. "I'm so glad you are here. If we didn't have so much work to do, I would retire and hand the job over to you and Jason." Her dad smiled. "I'm thankful your first two cases with Jason were resolved so well. We'll have dinner now if you're ready."

"I'm so glad to be here. And yeah, I'm definitely ready to celebrate."

"I'll meet you at the house. Why don't you ride with Jason? My car needs to be cleaned out before anyone can ride in it."

She couldn't believe her dad wouldn't have cleaned out his car so she could ride with him in his vehicle when he was *supposed* to have been picking her up at the airport and taking her to lunch earlier. It seemed like another convenient excuse to have her stay with Jason further.

But she was thinking about what her dad had said. That if he retired, he'd hand the agency over to her and Jason. Did he plan to make them equal partners in the business? That hadn't been in the plans.

She was supposed to be in charge someday, so she thought it just went without saying that when she had to work with Jason, she would be in charge even now. She took in a deep breath and let it out. Jason was used to doing things his way. And she was used to a whole different setup with working for the government so she just needed to switch gears and play the game for now. She hoped he would be easy to work with and not give her a hard time, like he did with telling her to watch the kids and he was going to help Brian free the snow leopard.

"I hope you don't mind driving me home since my dad has decided you will." She and Jason headed out to his car. "Though I do love the luxury ride."

Jason smiled at her. "It's no problem. I was headed that way anyway, and I still have your luggage in my car."

"Do you have dinner with my dad very often?" she asked, as they both climbed into the Jaguar.

"Sometimes, when we have cases we want to discuss with each other and don't want the interruptions at the office. Sometimes, I think he's just lonely."

She had kind of wondered about that. "What about a girl-friend? Don't you have any other plans?" She had thought she would be having dinners with her dad and that they wouldn't include Jason. Though she was glad that they had worked so well together so far and since this was a celebration and not just a dinner, she was glad Jason was joining them tonight.

"Are you asking because you're interested?" He gave her a smug smile.

"Hardly. I just hoped my dad wasn't expecting you to have dinner with him because he was lonely and needed compan-ionship."

"That's why you came home, right?"

"In part, yes. He wanted me to join the FBI, get some of their training and then come to work with him. But I'm here now, so I'll keep him company when he needs me to."

"So you don't have a boyfriend?"

"Why? Are *you* interested?"

He chuckled. "I just was giving you a hard time back."

"I did have a boyfriend in this area, but I have no idea if he's dating or mated or what." She had lost touch with him. He probably figured she'd never leave the FBI and live here, so why bother with her? She had to admit, they hadn't really had the chemistry to make her want to move here any sooner than she had.

They finally arrived at her dad's house and went inside to start the meal. Jason made them pina coladas while her dad headed outside to start the grill and Erin peeled potatoes to make the mashed potatoes. "Go visit with Dad. Help him with whatever he needs help with."

It was too chilly to actually eat outside though.

She heard them talking about going fishing and hadn't expected to see this side of Jason. They were even planning to take her with them. She was an excellent fisherman, as long as she was in her jaguar coat. Jaguars thoroughly enjoyed swimming too. She loved how her dad had an indoor pool and she planned to swim in it later once Jason had gone home for the night.

When they finally finished grilling the steaks and she'd made the side dishes, they put the food on the table and sat down to eat.

"I'm glad the case of the missing kids turned out well," Cannon said.

"Yeah, I never expected for the case to involve a bunch of shifters and then that anyone would have to turn the ones who were human too," Jason said.

"That's what I was thinking," Erin said.

During the meal, she shared FBI stories that she hadn't told her dad yet and they informed her about some of the cases they'd had to solve.

The steaks and cheesy broccoli and mashed potatoes all had

turned out great. But then her dad said, "Hey, I've got to run in to do some surveillance work."

She frowned at him. "Tonight? Okay, so what do you need me to do?"

"If you don't mind, clean the dishes and Jason will take care of the grill and will help you clean whatever you don't get to. Then the two of you are going to go swimming and I'll be back in about an hour to join you."

She was thinking her dad was trying to set her up big time with Jason.

Before she could object, her dad was out the door. She couldn't believe how spry he could be when he was on a mission, though he was a big cat and all of them were mobile and agile. Jason looked like he was ready for whatever her dad had cooked up. "I'll go clean up the grill."

Then Jason disappeared outside, and she began to put away the dishes and work on the pans she had used for cooking. Then she wondered what Jason was going to swim in!

When Jason came back inside, Erin said, "I think the party tomorrow night will be fun. I've never been to the billionaire's mansion."

"Strom has a fantastic spread, great for parties and for running as jaguars. I'm sure everyone will get a kick out of the snow leopards."

Like Strom, her father lived out in the country, and it was really private out there. Essentially, they could wear, or not wear, anything they wanted to swim in. Maybe Jason could wear his underwear. She hoped to run as a jaguar tonight also.

When she was halfway through cleaning up the dishes, Jason had gone out to his car and brought in all her bags and set them in her bedroom for her. Then he joined her in the kitchen and grabbed up the other pan and started to clean it. Now this, she could get used to. "Thanks for bringing in my bags. So did you bring a swimsuit?" she asked him.

"A swimsuit?"

"To swim in? You are going swimming, right?"

"Yeah, if you want to."

"I'd love to get some exercise after all the traveling I did today and of course being busy with the cases we handled."

"What about a run in the woods as a jaguar?" Jason asked.

"Yes! I'd love to." She had thought she would run alone if her dad wasn't going to be around. "Do you think he's really working on the case tonight, or seeing more of Laura?"

"He's really a workaholic and dedicated to his missions."

"Yeah, I know, but do you think he'll be seeing more of her?"

"I do."

Erin glanced at Jason. "I should have told my dad to invite her over tonight to enjoy the dinner with us."

"I think your dad wanted to wait a bit since you just got here and maybe ease you into this or even just get his feet wet with her first, so to speak. He might not even be sure if he's ready for anything with her either."

"You're right." Then she sighed. "You're nothing like I expected." She had to admit that to Jason. When she'd popped in to see her dad on holidays and for his birthday and hers, she would see Jason for brief periods. He had been short with her and didn't seem friendly at all. Like he was afraid she'd break up his friendship with her dad or something. But she had really been glad Jason had been there for her dad when he had needed the help. And she was glad they were more than just a boss and his employee. They were friends. And a friend of her father's was a friend of hers. Usually. At least it was a lot easier to like someone who was nice to her dad.

"What did you expect?" Jason continued to scrub the pan.

"You were always kind of abrupt with me when I came in to see my dad."

Jason set the pan down on the drying pad on the counter. "I was always busy with a job."

"Uh-uh. You were busy, sure, but you weren't friendly, and that was evident. It would have been easy enough to just cast a smile my way and—"

"Kiss you?" He pulled her into his arms.

She wasn't expecting this. This time they weren't undercover. He leaned down to kiss her, and she lifted her head to press her kisses against his mouth. Warm, willing, eager.

He gave her mouth a little lick, then kissed her again and she melted against him, for heaven's sake.

Then he released her. "Your dad adores you and he wanted you to do what you were happy with doing, but he desperately wanted you home. Not only because he missed you terribly, but he wanted you working with him in the business. He worried you might get hurt while working with the FBI. I...I'm sorry. I guess I was just angry with you for not being able to see that."

She was stunned. "He never once acted like he wanted me home. He continually said how proud he was that I was working for the FBI." She let out her breath. "Well, how do you feel about me now?"

"You're home, he's happy, I'm happy. And I think we're going to make a great team. I wasn't sure, but after we did such a great job on Henry and Samantha's cases, I'd say, yeah, we're going to do all right."

She had been worried about that. About working with a PI who was close to her father but could barely tolerate her. She hadn't realized why he'd felt such animosity toward her, but now she could.

"Well, I really didn't know, or I would have quit my job sooner. I wanted to, actually, but Dad just kept praising me for a job well done that I thought he wasn't ready for me to come home and work with him."

"That's because he was proud of what you'd been doing with the FBI, and he was afraid you wouldn't be satisfied with just PI cases. I guess I should have talked to you about it. I just didn't want to come between you and your father."

"Or mess up your special relationship with him either."

"Yeah, there was that. He's been like a father to me since I began working for him. You can't know how much that means to me after losing my own parents earlier on."

"I understand." Then she frowned at him. "At the zoo today, I was going to go with the wolf to free his friend, not stay with the kids, but you took over and told me how the situation was going to be handled."

"Sorry. I knew you wanted to help free the man. It's in our blood to want to rescue shifters in need. But I could also see Samantha didn't want you to leave her. She needed answers about our kind."

"Ha! Dale shamed you into going in my place."

Jason smiled and the look he gave her told her that wasn't his reasoning at all.

"Samantha did seem grateful that she was able to talk to me about the jaguar business," Erin admitted.

"I knew she would. Woman to woman."

"So how are you dressing for swimming?" she asked him again.

"I've got my swimsuit. I always bring it when I come to your dad's place so I can swim."

"Oh, good. I'll grab mine then and we can meet at the pool."

Then she headed for the bedroom and went inside the room to change into her bathing suit. She dressed in her one-piece, blue swimsuit and left the room to join Jason. He was already waiting for her on the pool patio.

He looked sexy, hunky, all his muscle groups toned—not muscle bound, but just right. He was looking her over too, smiling, such a change from when she'd visited before. Though they'd both gotten an eyeful of each other at the Potters' house when they had shifted to show off their jaguar coats to the Potter family.

Then she said, "I'll race you to the other side." She dove into the pool and began swimming. He was in the pool and beside her in a minute. She couldn't believe he'd swim that fast. She should have realized he could, being a jaguar.

Still, it startled her and she tried to reach the end but he got there before her and when she reached the end, he smiled. "I could have let you win, but I figured you wanted to beat me without me giving in."

"You are fast."

"I was a swimming champion in high school."

"Ha! You could have told me that first. I was homeschooled. My parents figured I would be too growly if I had gone to public or private school."

He smiled at her, then his expression turned contemplative. "I didn't have a choice. My foster parents were human so I had to deal with it. It wasn't easy at times, believe me. Some big kids thought they could bully me, but I'd taken martial arts and wrestling and then swimming, so I was in good shape. They were just lucky I didn't resort to being a jaguar. Then see how big a bully they could be against one of our kind."

"Oh, I'm sorry. I didn't know that."

"Thanks, I learned to live with it."

She wished her father had told her about that. "I'll race you again." She took off and again, he gave her a head start and beat her by a foot. She sighed. She probably would never beat him at the game of swimming, but she had fun trying. And she wasn't giving up.

This time, he pulled her into his arms. Now this, she hadn't expected either. "Don't you think it might be frowned upon if the boss sees his employees fraternizing?" she asked.

"I think this was what your dad has been hoping for all along."

She sighed. "Well, just think of it this way, if you had been friendlier when I visited before, I might very well have figured I should have left the FBI to be with you."

He chuckled. "I think both your dad and I had goofed then."

"I agree. So you're not seeing anyone?"

"No. I had to give you a chance to prove you were an interesting jaguar to date."

"Oh, really."

"Yeah. I've waited a long time to find that out."

"You said you use your hot car to pick up women."

"On the rare occasion I've dated. Your dad has kept me working long hours."

"Hopefully, I can take up some of the workload and we can still see each other on the side."

* * *

ERIN LICKED the water off his neck, and Jason kissed the top of her head. Then they were kissing again, and he hoped her dad wasn't coming home anytime soon. If they could play together as well as they worked together, it worked for him. Right now, he was glad they were swimming in the heated pool. They deepened the kiss and he realized she was a lot more into him than he had suspected. He guessed his annoyance with her when she first saw him during visits with her dad hadn't dissuaded her from getting to know Jason.

Jason had decided, once he'd seen how Erin could be when she was sticking around, that he was dating her. He hoped things would work out between them because if they did, he wouldn't be looking for another job when her dad retired, he'd be mated to her, and they'd run the agency together. He'd like that.

He had really enjoyed the time he'd already spent with her and hoped she was enjoying the same with him. She seemed to. She'd always made an effort to be friendly toward him, but he'd been upset with her for not just leaving her job and joining her father. Because of that, he'd had a hard time dealing with it. He knew it all had to do with her being lucky enough to still have a father and that she was throwing that connection with her dad away. Anyway, now Jason was glad she was home, and things were really looking up.

He kissed her again, his erection already growing with his desire for her building. She was soft in all the right places, fit against him nicely, and her kissing him was just as eager and hungry as his kissing her was. He was amused she thought she could beat him at swimming, but she wasn't the kind of woman who wanted him to give her the win just because he was trying to get on her good side.

"Do you...uhm, think my dad was hoping this would happen between us?"

"Yeah. I mean, I didn't expect him to leave, or have me pick you up at the airport, or have you eat with me instead of him doing so, but after he kept changing the game plan and it meant I was spending more time with you, even on the cases we had today, I figured then that was his plan."

She brushed a wet curl off her cheek. "He's with Laura." Then she frowned. "Do you think he's staying with her the night?"

Jason smiled. "Maybe. He's dedicated to his mission when he starts one."

Erin groaned. "Come on. Let's swim some more, then run as jaguars."

"Okay."

They started swimming, him chasing her and tackling her in the water, and then she'd turn around and get him. Suddenly, he pulled off his swim trunks, laid them on the pool patio, and shifted into the jaguar. She laughed. Her cheerful laugh cheered him.

He came after her and she struggled to get out of her bathing suit, tossed it up on the patio and shifted right before he tackled her. Then he had a hold of her neck and was mouthing her like a big cat in play, and she nuzzled him and did the same thing with him, mouthing his neck in a playful bite. She turned around to capture his tail. He growled at her, and she growled back at him.

He hadn't played with a she-cat like this in forever. And she wasn't holding back. She bit at his flank underwater, and he dove around and under to bite her. They came up for air and she licked the water off his face. He did the same with her and they left the water at the same time, leaping out of the pool onto the patio with a single bound. They raced off toward the door to the yard and pushed through it. He followed her. They ran through the woods on her dad's acreage then.

They raced each other, her leaping into a tree and him following, then she would leap down just as fast, and he'd miss being with her on the branch. But sometimes she would leap onto a branch, and he would anticipate her jumping off the branch, and be ready to chase after her. This time, she swiped at him and knocked him out of the tree. He landed on his feet, naturally, but he was so surprised she had changed tactics.

Then the race was on again. She was an incredibly fast runner, even for a jaguar, a beautiful golden jaguar, not like him. He was black with rosettes visible in certain lights. He had never anticipated having so much fun with her like this. Or planning to do anything but watch a movie tonight—by himself. He figured Erin and her dad would have been just sharing family time.

Then she came to a pond and dove in, and he chased after her, back to water play. He didn't want the night to end he was having such a great time. He hoped she didn't want it to either.

CHAPTER 9

*S*now began to fall as Jason and Erin raced back to the house in their jaguar coats. Erin wanted to do this again with Jason tomorrow night at Strom's mansion, if he was game and they weren't investigating another high-priority case.

The temperature was really dropping by the time they finally reached the house, and they dove through the jaguar door leading to the indoor swimming pool. They crossed the pool patio and returned to where they'd left their wet bathing suits and a stack of towels were sitting on a bench for their use. They shifted, then wrapped themselves in towels. Then they grabbed up their wet bathing suits and went inside the house.

"That was fun," she said. "I haven't done that in a while. It's kind of hard to do it on missions and finding a safe place to run could be difficult too."

"Yeah, that's another reason I like working for your dad. This place is perfect for jaguar runs through the woods."

"Do you get to do it very often?"

"No. When we're not really busy, we try to get a jaguar run in though."

"Maybe with three of us working cases, we'll all have more

time for fun. Man, is it getting cold out there," Erin said. "I'll be out in a minute." She went into her bedroom and pulled on her panties, jeans, a bra, a warm sweater, and slipper boots, and set her damp towel in the laundry room where his was already hanging.

Then she walked into the living room where Jason was dressed in the clothes he had worn earlier, and he'd already started a fire. She really appreciated that he was always proactive.

"It's been two hours since Dad left and he's not back yet." She checked her text messages and phone messages. "He didn't let me know he was returning any time soon. Did you want something hot to drink? Like peppermint cocoa?" She pulled out a box of some peppermint cocoa.

"Yeah, sure, that would be great. I'm sure he just got—"

"Sidetracked with Laura?" Belatedly, she realized she should have just pulled on some lounge pants and a shirt, instead of getting fully dressed. She wanted to relax, but she did have company. Then she called her dad to make sure he was all right.

"Hey, Dad, the weather is getting worse. When are you going to be home?"

"The roads are really icy out here. I'm staying put for the night. Tell Jason not to drive anywhere either. Have him put the Jag in the garage. It looks like it's really going to get bad," her dad said.

In the past six years, they'd had snow here three of those years —nothing substantial, but weirder weather out of the norm was becoming the norm. Still, it hadn't been that bad. They'd had about half an inch to three inches of snow—fun for sharing photos with friends in other parts of the States, mostly up north, who were as unused to seeing them have snow as they were.

"You're staying at Laura's?" Erin asked her dad.

"Uh, yeah, she's putting me up for the night."

Erin's jaw dropped. She really was surprised. Had her dad been seeing her for some time then? She hoped her dad didn't think that Jason was supposed to entertain her while he dated Laura. And she hoped her dad hadn't been hiding that he'd been dating Laura, afraid to let on to Erin about it. "Okay, well don't do anything I wouldn't."

Her dad just laughed, and she smiled, figuring her dad would do whatever he wanted. He always did, and it was all right with her. He sounded like he was ready to move on with his life, and she was glad for that. She glanced at Jason who was waiting to hear what was going on. "Night, Dad, see you tomorrow then."

"Not if the weather is bad. Don't go anywhere."

"All right." She knew they'd all be at work tomorrow. She didn't figure the weather would be all that bad or last that long either. She set her phone on the kitchen island counter. "Okay, Dad's staying at his girlfriend's place for the night because he thinks the snow and ice will be too hazardous for driving conditions. He wants you to stay here tonight because the roads are getting icy." She turned on the TV to see the updates on the news, not believing it could be that dangerous.

To her surprise, and Jason's, several pileups of vehicles on the highways and roads had already occurred. She was so glad her dad wasn't coming home.

"Okay, you're staying the night," she said to Jason, not wanting to be responsible for his safety if he were to decide to try and brave the weather on the way home in his fancy Jaguar. She hoped he would be fine with staying here with her. "Oh, and Dad said to move your car into the garage for safekeeping."

He smiled, looking perfectly pleased with the notion.

"You didn't have anything to do with any of this, did you?" she asked, giving him a mug of peppermint cocoa.

He chuckled. "No. I have nothing to do with the weather, but I wouldn't have been entirely surprised if Cannon had decided to stay with Laura tonight anyway and we would have been left to our own—"

"Mischief?"

"Yeah. I'll park the car in the garage and be right back." He set his mug of cocoa on the coffee table and hurried out to get his car while she opened the garage door for him. Once he had parked it safely inside, she closed the garage door and they returned to the house.

She sat down with Jason on the couch and turned the TV to another channel. "Do you want to watch a movie?" She felt it was too early to go to bed, though she was happily tired. With the flight and all the other activities she'd been involved in today, she just wanted to relax, though she had never believed she would be sitting on the couch with Jason watching a movie and not with her dad. Not to mention that Jason would be staying the night with her instead of her dad.

The home had two bedrooms, her dad's master bedroom and Erin's bedroom. He had two more bedrooms, but one was used as an office and the other was just filled with stuff. She was hoping to help him clean it out and maybe turn it into her own office where she could work when she wasn't at the office.

Jason could sleep on the couch, but she was leaning toward inviting him into her bed. Was she being impulsive, or what? But she'd had such a good time with him today, and she really wanted to take this further. Her dad liked him. Jason seemed to be a really likeable guy now that he was working with her.

They watched a thriller, and they even cuddled up together on the couch. This was so nice. When the movie was over, she hesitated to mention offering her bed to him. Would he think she was moving too fast?

He rubbed her back and she said, "Okay, you have a choice, my bed or the couch."

"Hell, that's not really much of a choice." He smiled at her and leaned down and kissed her, but before they got carried away on the couch, they made sure the fire was out, turned off the television, and then they headed for her bedroom.

He wasn't asking if she was sure of this, and though she was, she was glad he didn't say anything to make her doubt herself. No, he was just as eager to move the bar forward.

The hour was late when he removed his shoes and socks next to the bed while she pulled off her slippers. Their gazes collided, his warm smile softening his features. His sturdy jaw was covered in whiskers, and he was devastatingly gorgeous.

He cupped her sweater-covered breasts and she wished again that she had worn just her lounge pants and shirt and she wasn't wearing her bra and panties.

But they'd quickly remedy that. He kissed her mouth, his hands sliding up her sweater to cup her breasts. His hands swept around to her back, and he unfastened her bra.

That was a unique feeling. To be free of her bra, but still be wearing both her bra and her sweater. But she forgot all of that when his hands moved back to her breasts and he cupped them, kneading them, making her nipples peak to his touch. Oh, this was...*heavenly.*

She inserted her tongue into his mouth to stroke his and he sucked on it, making her panties wet. She was so ready for him. He removed his hands from her breasts, and she wanted to protest until she realized he was going to pull off her sweater and bra. Once he'd dispensed with them, he moved his mouth to one breast, one of his hands keeping the other breast company.

Her knees weakened and she slid her hands down to his belt and began to unfasten it. She'd heard that wolf shifters mated for life when they had consummated sex. Not so for the big cats...so she wasn't waiting.

She slid her fingers down his zipper, then unfastened his pants and pulled down his zipper. His arousal was already full and pressing heavily against his clothes for release. He was well-endowed, his name, Biggerstaff, suiting him. Even though she knew the name was English, she'd had to look up the meaning because a girlfriend had said his name must be based on him having a large...staff. Erin found that it possibly meant beekeeper based on a village similarly named, or a bicker staff, a quarter staff used in a skirmish.

But yeah, he was impressive.

Once he had kicked off his pants the rest of the way, he removed her pants. He moved her to the bed. She had never expected to be having sex with him in her bed at her dad's home. Especially not on her first day back home.

But this all felt right—him, her, the two of them together like this.

She began yanking his boxer briefs down, wanting to see every glorious inch of him. He pulled off her panties last. For a moment, they both eyed each other as if measuring them up to see if they had all the attributes necessary to encourage them to make a lasting bond—a wild animal's approach to mating.

Then they were kissing again. He spread her legs and began to work on her clit, touching, stroking, teasing the sensitive flesh. Until she was aching for him. She closed her eyes, barely breathing, soaking in the erotic sensations filling her with desperate need.

Before she could come, he moved his body between her legs and pressed his *bigger staff* deep, causing her body to stretch to accommodate his size. He began to thrust, slowly at first, gaining momentum, plunging deep. She was so close to coming, he soon pushed her right over the edge. She cried out, the orgasm hitting her all at once. She shattered in exquisite ecstasy, and she was so ready to do this again in a few hours!

Her hands swept over his thrusting hips, his body well-toned, meant for loving, his muscles rippling with the erotic exercise. A rush of warmth filled her whole body as he plunged harder, faster. His gaze smoldering, he kissed her again, his dark eyes unfathomable, sexy, mesmerizing.

His body pressed against hers, making hers sizzle and she didn't want this to end. Their pheromones were on fire, the adrenaline fired up, but she reminded herself it wouldn't have to be the last time. This was just the beginning.

She dragged his face back to hers and kissed him wantonly, telling him in no uncertain terms, he had her attention, all of it, and she wanted more.

Then he came in an explosive finale, and she felt the aftershocks running through her body and gloried in the feeling of their union.

He collapsed on top of her, like a heavy, protective blanket of hard muscles and heat. She wrapped her arms around him, keeping him locked in place. Until she finally kissed his cheek and he moved off her, pulling the covers over them. She thought he might want to separate from her because neither of them was used to sleeping with someone else.

But right away, he pulled her close and she melted against him. This felt right. Better than right. And she was already wondering what his home was like because she didn't think she'd be able to do this again with Jason, if she did this again, if her dad were at home at the same time.

"This is the best day of my life," he said, kissing the top of her head and she was feeling the very same way.

"Yeah, the best day ever. *And* the best night."

CHAPTER 10

*T*he next morning, Jason woke and ran his hand over Erin's silky hair. Her arm and leg were draped over his body, but her breathing and heart rate were steady. She was still sound asleep. He kissed Erin's head, glad for the beautiful evening they'd shared, and he hoped Cannon and Laura's evening had been just as nice. Erin didn't stir, so Jason carefully slid out from under her so as not to wake her so he could take a shower. He got into the shower and started washing up, wishing he'd had a change of clothes. He'd spent an incredible night with her, and he was really glad her dad hadn't come home so that Jason and Erin had had all the privacy they had needed in the world. After they had some breakfast, he intended to go home to change into some fresh clothes. But then he realized Erin would need a ride into the office. She could go with him to his home.

When he dressed, he found Erin was still sleeping. She was probably worn out after waking him in the middle of the night so they could make love to each other again. Unexpected, but totally welcome.

He went into the living room, curious if they had any snow on the ground from last night's "snowstorm" and glanced out the window. At least a foot and a half of snow had buried the grass and covered all the vegetation from the pine and live oak trees to the evergreen holly and boxwood shrubs. He closed his gaping mouth shut. That's when he realized the house was way colder than it should have been.

With a jaguar's excellent night vision, he could see in the low light of the house, and he hadn't turned on any lights. He flipped a light switch on in the living room and nothing happened. He tried a couple of more light switches in the kitchen. The lights were out. They had no electricity.

Jason texted Cannon right away: *Electric's out here. What about where you're at?*

Cannon texted back: *Out here too. There are accidents everywhere. Enjoy a break today. Feel free to use any of my clothes until you can return home. Don't chance going home in this.*

The Houston area just wasn't geared to handle the roads for the kind of deep freeze they were in, not like northern states could deal with it.

Jason texted back: *Are you going to be all right?*

Yeah, Laura has a fireplace, gas stovetop, and we can cook on the stovetop at least. So can you. Make yourself at home.

Jason wondered if Erin's father had guessed just how much Jason had made himself at home already. He went into the living room and started a fire. At least that would help to heat the living room up a bit.

"Brr, why is it so cold in here?" Erin asked, joining him in the living room. She was wearing a heavy, blue sweater, jeans, and fluffy, butternut-colored slipper boots, looking perfectly huggable.

"The electricity is out. I called Cannon's electric service and it's out all over the area."

"You're kidding."

"No, and I'm sorry. I took a shower already, but there should be enough hot water for you to take one. I didn't realize we didn't

DAWN OF THE JAGUAR

have any electricity at the time, or I would have waited until after you had your shower first."

"Oh, no problem. I appreciate you saying so though. If we had known this would happen, we could have showered last night. Thanks for starting a fire." Then she headed for the bathroom.

After a very quick shower, she was dressed and headed for the living room, trying to towel dry her hair. She moved a big pillow onto the floor to sit on in front of the fire to help dry her hair the rest of the way. "Okay, so do we have electricity at the office?"

"We can't get in because of the snow and ice."

"No. Way." She got back up and looked out the window. "Ohmigod, this is unreal." She grabbed her phone and headed outside to take pictures. But she didn't last long outside in the cold and hurried back inside. "What about Dad? Are he and Laura okay?"

"He's at Laura's house and they've got a fire going in the fireplace. He said they have a gas stovetop there, and since we have one here, we can all still cook meals."

"Oh, sure, that's good. Well, this is all so unexpected."

"You must have brought the bad weather with you from Maryland."

She smiled at him. "My coworkers always said that when we were having a heatwave here and I returned to Maryland where they were having one also, that I'd brought it back from Texas after visiting my dad."

He laughed. "I'm just glad you flew in yesterday when you did."

"So you would have company today?"

"Yeah, it worked out great for me for sure." He smiled and pulled her into his arms. She was chilled from the cold air outside, and her hair was still damp. He kissed her nose. "Would you like tea or coffee?"

"I'll have tea. I can make the hot water for my tea if you want to mix up some coffee in a saucepan of hot water and make yours that way. You can get the fireplace gas lighter to light the stovetop burners." In the meantime, she pulled out the coffee and a teabag and brought out a couple of jaguar-decorated mugs.

He lit the stovetop burners and then they started heating the water for their coffee and tea.

She began looking in the fridge to see what they could have for breakfast. "Eggs, bacon or sausage?"

"Eggs and sausages would be good."

"Ooh, Dad has frozen hash browns. We've got to have those too."

Jason smiled at her. He was enjoying learning more about Erin's personal habits. And he was already thinking of her staying with him and he was going to make sure he had hashbrowns on hand.

Then he got a call and left the kitchen to get his phone from the living room. He grabbed it off the coffee table and saw that it was Dale and he wondered what was up. "Hi, this is Jason. What can I do for you?"

"Samantha's having a fight with her mother over moving in with Henry's family," Dale said, as if Jason could do anything about it. "I mean, her mom doesn't even care if she's there or not. Not really. So why does her mom want to make a big deal of it? For the first time in her life, Samantha's really happy about this."

"I'm glad Samantha is. I'm not sure there's anything I can do about it." Jason wished he could, but his hands were really tied.

A lengthy silence ensued. "Samantha suddenly doesn't think she can be my girlfriend any longer."

Oh. So that was the real issue that was bothering Dale. Jason watched as Erin made breakfast when he had planned to help her. "I'm going to put this on speaker so Erin can listen in and offer advice if she has any to give."

Erin glanced at him, brows raised.

"It's Dale and he says Samantha's breaking up with him."

"Yeah," Dale said, "and both of you were there with her when she went to see the Potters. Did she say anything to either of you about me? Like, she thought I was a bad influence on her or something?"

No, it all had to do with her being a jaguar and realizing she needed to be with her own kind, Jason suspected. "No. But this is going to be a big adjustment to her," Jason said, trying to reassure Dale it had nothing to do with him. "Especially if her mother is making waves about her living with the Potters. I can imagine her mom feels they're saying she's not capable of taking care of Samantha and that isn't sitting well with her mom."

Erin agreed.

"Not only that, but her mom's boyfriend, Pete? He's a nice guy. The one who always stuck up for Samantha? Well, her mother had had enough of him going along with Samantha's plan to move in with the Potters and she dumped him," Dale said.

"Okay, so the only one who is on Samantha's side in her mother's home is gone then," Jason said.

"Yeah."

"It'll work out for Samantha." Jason couldn't say it would work out for Dale. Most likely Everett and Demetria had told Samantha what to expect with being one of their kind and that they didn't want her turning Dale. That he couldn't know what they were, and she should probably call it quits with him.

She might not have even been that into him, though he seemed to be a pretty nice guy, worried about her cousin, helping her out all the way.

"Samantha's mother didn't care if we were dating, now Samantha's aunt and uncle do?" Dale was clearly distraught. It sounded as though he wished she still lived with her mother, even if that wasn't the best situation for Samantha—especially given what Samantha was.

"We'll talk to her," Erin said. "You seem like a really good friend and both Jason and I commented on that to each other about how much you had helped her to recover her cousin and gave her all the support that you did. She's going through a rough time right now. But we'll both definitely talk to her."

"Okay, thanks." Dale didn't sound real hopeful it would help, but if he hadn't believed they might be able to assist him, why call them? Just to get it off his chest? Or did he hope they knew why she was trying to end things with him and wouldn't tell him herself. Which was certainly the case.

"We're going to grab some breakfast and then we'll check with her," Jason said.

"Okay." Then Dale ended the call, sounding totally distressed.

"I feel for him." Erin served up their breakfast while Jason got silverware for them and poured glasses of orange juice.

"Yeah, I do too. But you know they might just be friends and he's seeing more into their relationship than she is." Jason sat down with Erin at the maple dining table to eat.

"I agree. I just wish there was a way we could tell Dale that it's not him that's the problem. That she just can't be around him because of what she is. But you know what I want to do?"

Jason shook his head and forked up some of his hash browns. "Don't tell me. You want to investigate his family's background and see if he would make a likely candidate to be a jaguar shifter too."

"Actually, I want to learn how Samantha truly feels about him. I mean, if she's not that interested in him, then no. But if she is and really wants to continue to see him, I wouldn't mind checking out his family."

"Well, the problem is that even if she really cares for him, does that translate into a long-term desire to be with him? They're young. Seventeen, both of them. They have their whole lives ahead of them. I'd hate to turn him, even if they are totally infatuated with each other now, and then they have a falling out and look what we've done? Adding yet another jaguar to our shifter population who wouldn't have been turned otherwise. She's glad she is one of us, so is H.P, and from the sounds of it, so are

Henry's parents. But would Dale be happy with it if he was turned?"

"True." Erin finally finished the rest of her breakfast. "Okay, so we aren't going into the office today. First thing on the agenda for me is I'm calling Samantha to get her take on her boyfriend and learn what's up with the family situation."

"All right. I'm going to get hold of our lawyer and have him subpoena records for a client of mine and we'll compare notes later."

"Okay. You can use my laptop by the fire. I don't have it set up with the passwords and such though for the agency."

"I can set it up for you."

"Okay, thanks. And then I think I'll go ahead and unpack my clothes. Oh, and if you want, you can wash your clothes. Uhm, no, I guess you can't. Not until the electricity comes back on. You can borrow some things of Dad's."

Jason smiled. "Sure thing. He mentioned it already." Luckily, they were about the same build, so no problem with that. But what he really wanted to do was spend more quality time with Erin.

CHAPTER 11

*W*hile Jason was catching up on paperwork and doing some employment investigations, Erin called Samantha. "Hey, Samantha, Dale called and said you were having problems with your mom over moving in with your aunt and uncle."

"Yeah, but Everett and Demetria said you all have a lawyer and a judge who can help me get it approved."

"That's good news. Dale also said you were breaking up with him."

Samantha sighed. "He's not a jaguar and Demetria and Everett both said I need to meet one of my own kind instead."

"How do you feel about it?"

"I have mixed feelings. Turning my aunt and uncle I felt was necessary for Henry's safety. Besides, he kept telling me he was going to turn them. I didn't want him to have that on his conscience since I always felt bad that I had done that to him. I'm not sure how Dale would feel about it if we turned him, but I don't want to be responsible for it either. As much as I really care for him, I don't know. Would it change his feelings toward me?

With Henry, turning him brought us closer to each other, more so than we already were. I just don't know about Dale."

"What about his parents?"

"He's an emancipated teen."

Now that shed a different light on Dale's situation. Not that it meant they should turn him, but it could mean they wouldn't have to turn anyone else but Dale, if it was something everyone agreed to.

"Okay, well, for now, we'll leave things as they are."

* * *

THAT NIGHT, they were supposed to have the big party at Strom's place, but conditions were too icy still, roads closed, and a power outage was being felt all over Texas with the temperatures staying in the teens.

That meant the swimming pool was no longer being heated and too cold to swim in comfortably as humans. Though they could swim in it as jaguars. Instead, Jason and Erin went back to bed for lots more loving, no need for electricity for that.

* * *

FOR A WEEK, the freezing temperatures and death toll in the state rose as the electricity hadn't been restored for nearly all that time for many areas. By Friday, the lights finally came on in the living room where Jason had turned them on the morning that he had discovered they had no electricity.

"Wash clothes!" Erin immediately said and hurried to do a load of wash—just in case they lost the electricity again. She and Jason began gathering her clothes, his, and her dad's clothes that Jason had worn. "I wonder what my dad has been using for clothes all this time." She shoved the clothes into the wash machine, added detergent, and started the wash.

"I suspect he was prepared."

"He had a bag packed?" Now that surprised Erin.

"Yeah." Jason pulled her into his arms and kissed her. "You know when he returns, it will be kind of awkward with us in his house if we continue to make love with each other."

It felt like they'd been on a pre-honeymoon trip as they made love anytime they wanted to, got up when they wanted, took naps whenever they needed. And she had loved every bit of it, not having expected to be on "vacation" with a veritable hunk of a jaguar.

Her laptop battery had died and so had both their cellphones earlier in the week so they were unable to do much else but play boardgames and enjoy each other's company. Except that the client Jason had been dealing with concerning his ex-wife wanting alimony said she dropped the whole thing, and the client was forever indebted to him.

"Unless you want to go home with me at night," Jason said, looking hopeful.

She smiled up at him and ran her hands up his chest. "Yeah, that works for me. You know, I have fallen hopelessly in love with you." No way did she want to make boisterous love to Jason in the house when her dad was there. Their hearing was just too good. "Oh," she pulled away from him. "We've got to charge up the phones and my laptop."

"Wait." He caught up with her and dragged her tight against his body. "You can't drop that bombshell and just leave me hanging like that. I think I've always been in lust with you and fighting my natural instincts when it came to you—since you were not returning home for good."

"And then?"

"I fell in love with you, head over heels. I treasure you. You just take my breath away."

She smiled at him and squeezed him tight against her. "Good, because I thought you might need convincing after we got back to the business of investigating cases."

"Nah, I'm already there."

"That's a good thing. And we'll have to do something about it." Right after she checked on her dad!

As soon as she plugged her phone in, she got a call from her dad, startling her. "Hey, are you okay, Dad?"

"Yeah. How are the two of you doing?"

Jason was waiting beside her to hear what her dad had to say.

"Oh, we're good. We just got our electricity back."

"Same here."

"Jason will be going home. I'm sure he's ready to wear his own clothes again. You probably feel the same way about coming home."

"I'm...uh, going to stay here a while longer. A couple of weeks at least. I'll see you two on Monday for work."

That shocked her to the core. "Are you sure?"

"Yeah. We're getting some lunch now. I'll talk to you later."

"Okay. Bye, Dad." She thought she should have been disappointed to come home to spend more time with her dad just to learn he had found someone else to spend his time with. "Well, Dad said he's staying with Laura for a couple more weeks." And Erin *wasn't* disappointed.

Jason looked worried she'd be upset, but she smiled and led him into the kitchen to have lunch. "That means you can stay here with me for a couple more weeks so we can swim in the pool and run on the property and when he comes home, we can stay at your home, if you want."

Jason ran his hand over her hair. "Why don't you come to my place after lunch then and I'll pack up some things. Then you can see my place too."

"That's a deal."

After lunch, and on the way to Jason's place, she got a call from

Samantha. "Hi, my mom has decided she doesn't care if I live with the Potters, and she's taken her boyfriend Pete back. I'm thrilled. He is the nicest boyfriend she's ever had, and I really like him too."

"Oh, that's wonderful news." Though Erin definitely heard a "but" coming.

"But...well." Samantha let out her breath. "I can't stop seeing Dale. I really do care about him. He's always been there for me through all the turmoil in my life. He's devastated and...I took him back."

"Did you talk to Demetria and Everett about it?"

"Yes. They're involved in it. But I had to tell you."

"I totally understand. It will work out one way or another." At least Erin hoped it would all turn out the best for the both of them.

"Thanks. I'm not telling him about what we are or anything, but I just had to see him again."

"I trust you, Samantha. You and he will be fine." Despite Samantha being a kid, Erin really did trust she would keep their secret. Except for accidentally turning her cousin, she'd never exposed their kind to anyone else.

Jason encouraged Samantha too and then they arrived at his place and parked in the garage. They finally told her they'd keep in touch, ended the call, and they headed inside his home.

It was a really nice place, Erin thought. The walls were a pale gray, and the wraparound sectional sofas were a dark gray. He had a stone fireplace on one wall and a large screen TV on another. His kitchen had stainless-steel fixtures, and appliances, and the cabinets were all a slate blue. Very pretty.

She joined him in his bedroom while he packed. His bedroom featured a king-size bed, dark maple head and footboards, dressers, all ornate. She'd expected something more... modernistic, simple lines. Maybe because he owned the sleek Jaguar. But it really was nice. She checked out the bathroom while he was packing his clothes and liked how white everything was, making it appear larger—the sinks, the cabinetry, the glassed-in shower.

"What do you think?" he asked as he pulled a couple of suitcases he'd already tossed clothes into out of his bedroom and headed down the hall.

"I think when Dad returns to his house, this will do nicely."

He smiled at her. "I'm going to put these in the trunk of the car if you can grab my laptop."

"Got it," she said, grabbing it off his coffee table and carrying it out to the garage right behind him.

Once they packed up the car, he said, "I need to get my toiletry kit." He rubbed his whiskery jaw. "I'm getting to look a little rough."

"I like a little rough."

He chuckled.

When they were in the bedroom, she bounced on the bed and then laid back down. He came out of the bathroom with his toiletry kit in hand. She looked up at him. "Yeah, this will really do nicely when Dad returns to his home."

Jason moved like a jaguar after his prey, forget his toiletry kit, and set it on the bedside table. Then he settled his body on top of hers. "That's good news."

Then he was kissing her, and she was ready to try out his bed also when she heard a sound like the front door opening. She frowned at him, and he turned his head toward the sound also.

"Are you expecting anyone?" she whispered.

"No." He got off her without making a sound and carefully pulled a gun out of his bureau drawer.

She stripped off her clothes. He arched his brow at her. "Maybe I can chase the intruder off," she said, her voice hushed.

"Maybe he or they are armed with a gun." He had a good point.

"You go first."

He smiled at her, though she was certain he had meant to go first no matter what. And then she shifted.

Then he made his way down the hall, his gun readied, and she was right behind him as they heard three different people ransacking the living room. She wanted to scare them to pieces.

She was thinking they should have called 911, but it was too late for that. Then she remembered they couldn't have, because both their phones were sitting on the kitchen island.

"Hands up in the air!" Jason shouted, sounding like a police officer.

The three men stopped what they were doing, one tossing a couch cushion at Jason and pulling a gun. Instinctively—as a jaguar—Erin took a running leap and could actually make a jump forty-five-feet long. She landed on the gunman just as he fired, but the shot went into the ceiling. She swiped at his head—a little harder and it would have been a killing blow—but she only knocked him out.

The other men were dropping whatever they had in their hands and pulling guns out from their belts. Jason quickly shot the one man in the hand, forcing him to drop the gun he was aiming at Erin. She was on the move to take down the other guy, jumping over the couch in a single bound and leaped on top of him and took him to the floor. Like with the other man, she knocked him out with her powerful paw.

The wounded man raced for the door. Now that's what big cats liked. The chase. But she didn't have to chase him. She just leaped and pounced. Also what jaguars loved to do. Once she'd knocked him out, she licked Jason's hand, then headed back to the bedroom to shift and dress. Though she did like the idea of just getting naked and not having to dress again, she wasn't sure Jason would be in the mood for wild sex, and they had to talk to the police.

She sighed, but she only put on her shirt and pants, no underwear.

She heard Jason calling the police and she joined him in the living room, frowning at the mess these men had made. They all appeared to be in their twenties. Now this would be a crime scene for a while, which annoyed her to no end.

They heard sirens and Jason gave her a hug, his gun now on the kitchen counter. He would have to turn it over to the police for the time being. "Okay, so you know martial arts."

She smiled. "I certainly do. A double black belt in Ju Jitsu. I knocked out two of the men. You shot the one and then took him down with your own martial arts move." She knew Jason was also into martial arts. Which made her realize they needed to do that together too. How fun would that be? Sparring with each other. They did it as jaguars already and she loved it.

* * *

A CAR'S engine roared in the driveway and tires squealed while backing out in a hurry. Jason grabbed his phone and dashed out the door. He really hadn't thought these men would have a getaway driver. He took a picture of the speeding car and managed to get its license plate. Then the cops were pulling up in the driveway and he raised his hands, showing he was armed only with a phone, shouting he was the owner of the home, made the 911 call, and the getaway driver had just gotten away.

One of the cops got back into his patrol car and took off after the car they could see still heading down the street lickety split.

Then the police officers asked for Jason's ID, as he explained his girlfriend and PI partner at Big Cat Private Investigations Agency was inside, unarmed, and unharmed. "Erin is former FBI," he added, and he was damn thankful her jaguar moves had kept them both safe.

An ambulance drove up, and Jason went inside with the officers to explain what had happened.

"I was grabbing my toiletry kit in the bathroom when we heard what sounded like people ransacking the place," Jason said.

"And you didn't call us first?" one of the officers asked.

"Both our phones were on the kitchen counter. We'd been stuck at my dad's place during the ice storm," Erin said, "and we were returning there after picking up some of Jason's clothes."

"We'll need your gun," the officer said to Jason.

Jason motioned to the kitchen island where he'd placed it.

"Martial arts, eh?" the burglary detective said, walking into the house.

"Rocky Catskin, hell, when did you become a burglary detective here? I knew him on the force when I was a police officer. Both of us were, but then he got an assignment in Arizona," Jason told Erin. And he was a jaguar shifter just like them.

She smiled and shook Rocky's hand. "Good to meet you."

"I know some of those martial art moves," Rocky said. "We'll have to get some more practice in."

"That would be great."

"We'll need you to step outside while we take care of these men and document the crime scene," Rocky said.

Jason and Erin both knew the drill. They went outside and waited to talk to Rocky again.

When Rocky joined them, he said, "Sorry, man, but we have to maintain the crime scene for at least forty-eight hours."

"Can we take my car and drive to Erin's dad's place at least? We were just grabbing some of my clothes so we could do that," Jason said.

"Yeah, sure. The crime scene was confined to the living room. So go ahead and take the car."

"Hell, my toiletry kit is in the bedroom."

"And my bra and panties are on the floor next to the bed," Erin said.

Jason looked down at her and smiled. She looked up at him and smiled back.

Rocky was smiling too. "Uh, sorry, folks. If you have to go through the living room, you can't."

"No problem. We'll make do." Jason used the keypad on the garage door and opened it, then they got into the Jaguar, backed out of the garage, and he used the remote control to close the garage door back up. He rolled down his window to talk to Rocky. "We'll make a swimming pool date and a run through the woods with you within the next couple of weeks while we're staying at Erin's dad's place."

"Hey, that sounds like a winner," Rocky said.

Though Jason knew that Rocky might have a hard time finding the spare time to do it with all the burglary cases he'd have to deal with in the area.

* * *

THEN ROCKY DIRECTED a couple of officers to move their vehicles so Jason and Erin could leave, and she sighed with relief as she and Jason drove off. "Sorry about taking the men down as a jaguar."

"The EMTs said we should be boxers. Besides, if you hadn't taken the men down, we would have been dead. All three of the men were armed. They all had their guns out. They weren't going to hesitate to shoot—but you didn't give them the chance—courtesy of the power of the jaguar's leap. It was a perfect case of home invasion and self-defense."

"Right, but they'll all claim there's a jaguar living there that had injured them."

"Did you notice that they had all been drinking?"

"Yes, the smell of alcohol was present."

"Exactly. And they'll test them for blood alcohol levels. I smelled weed on them too. They might have been doing other drugs also. So, with the combination of those things, and the fact it was a lot easier to tell the story that a jaguar beat them up rather than a woman, I'd say that gets us off the hook." He reached over and took her hand in his and squeezed it in a loving way. "You know, I kind of wish I hadn't been picking you up to bring you home from the airport when you first arrived."

"Oh?"

"Yeah, I wish I'd been taking you on a trip to paradise instead."

She chuckled and pressed her head against his shoulder, loving him through thick and thin. "You know what? You already have."

And when they arrived at her dad's house, they were heading straight back to her bed to profess their love for one another... again. There wasn't any need to find paradise anywhere else. They'd found it right here together.

EPILOGUE

*E*rin loved her dad and she really cared about Laura too. She couldn't believe that her dad had given her and Jason his home while her dad moved in with Laura. Her dad and Laura were marrying at the end of the year. Once her dad had proved the manager of the restaurant had stolen from Laura's bank account and went to trial for it, she believed Erin's dad was a superhero.

Erin had always known that.

And with Erin and Jason staying at their "new" home, Jason rented out his own place.

Her dad wasn't retiring just yet. He still loved taking care of cases, but he was working fewer days per week so he could spend more time with Laura. Both Jason and Erin were happy for them. Her dad had finally revealed the reason he had thrown them together so much—and Laura had helped with it. Though the ice storm had sealed the deal. Erin's dad had known all along Jason and Erin had the hots for each other just from watching the interaction between them during Erin's visits, despite denying their interest in each other from the very beginning. Her dad had good cat instincts.

Now, Erin and Jason were running the Big Cat Private Investigations Agency together as partners. And after the day was done, they enjoyed the indoor swimming pool, sometimes with their shifter friends and family and other times, just the two of them alone. And running through the woods in their jaguar coats was a given.

They'd even finally managed to go to Strom's billionaire bash on his property, once the temperatures had warmed up and everyone had their electricity back. Even the police detective, Rocky, was there, and the Arctic wolf and the three snow leopards had made a special trip there, staying with Strom, but they had come at his request to show off their special fur coats to all the jaguars. Some of the gray wolves in the United Shifter Force were there too.

Erin and Jason had even returned to the zoo, this time with Dale, Samantha, and Henry, and Layla, Jason's sister, and her two children—Jason and Erin treating the whole lot to pizzas and cookies, but it wouldn't be the last time.

The situation with the burglars was resolved—the men had been responsible for several armed robberies across the city and beyond—and were held without bond for trial.

More than anything, Erin was glad she'd finally come home for good and found she had everything she'd needed in her life right there—a mate, her family, and all her friends, both the new and the old.

* * *

JASON WAS glad Erin had finally come home at the agency and he thought it was mostly for her dad's benefit. But working with her that first day and playing with her after that, Jason knew he was glad she had come home for *him*.

As to the snow leopard that had been found and turned over to the zoo and then had vanished, no one would ever be able to solve that mystery. Except the Big Cat Private Investigations Agency and friends who knew all about it and they were keeping mum about that.

And Henry and Samantha were as happy as could be with their newly turned jaguar family and all the new friends they'd made. After much consideration, it was agreed upon that Dale would be turned too and be trained as an intern in the JAG's United Shifter Force branch. He couldn't have been happier, and he and Samantha were still dating.

Most of all, Jason had found his mate in Erin, who wouldn't have had it any other way.

ACKNOWLEDGMENTS

Thanks so much to Donna Fournier and Darla Taylor for loving Dawn of the Jaguar and suggesting changes. When I bought the cover for this book, I was visiting Donna in Minnesota. On our way to see the wolves and bears in Ely, we were brainstorming the story—character names, a little of the plot. It changed, of course, but every time I worked on Dawn of the Jaguar, I thought fondly of all the fun we'd had!

AUTHOR BIO

USA Today bestselling author Terry Spear has written over a hundred paranormal and medieval Highland romances. In 2008, Heart of the Wolf was named a Publishers Weekly Best Book of the Year. She has received a PNR Top Pick, a Best Book of the Month nomination by Long and Short Reviews, numerous Night Owl Romance Top Picks, and 2 Paranormal Excellence Awards for Romantic Literature (Finalist & Honorable Mention). In 2016, Billionaire in Wolf's Clothing was an RT Book Reviews Top Pick. A retired officer of the U.S. Army Reserves, Terry also creates award-winning teddy bears that have found homes all over the world, helps out with her granddaughter and grandson, and she is raising two Havanese puppies. She lives in Spring, Texas.

For more information, please visit her website at: www.terryspear.com,

Blog: https://terryspearbooks.blog/

Follow her for new releases and book deals: www.bookbub.com/authors/terry-spear

Or follow her on Twitter, @TerrySpear.

Facebook: http://www.facebook.com/terry.spear.

ALSO BY TERRY SPEAR

Heart of the Cougar Series:

Cougar's Mate, Book 1

Call of the Cougar, Book 2

Taming the Wild Cougar, Book 3

Covert Cougar Christmas (Novella)

Double Cougar Trouble, Book 4

Cougar Undercover, Book 5

Cougar Magic, Book 6

Cougar Halloween Mischief (Novella)

Falling for the Cougar, Book 7

Catch the Cougar (A Halloween Novella)

Cougar Christmas Calamity Book 8

You Had Me at Cougar, Book 9

Saving the White Cougar, Book 10

Heart of the Bear Series

Loving the White Bear, Book 1

Claiming the White Bear, Book 2

The Highlanders Series: Winning the Highlander's Heart, The Accidental Highland Hero, Highland Rake, Taming the Wild Highlander, The Highlander, Her Highland Hero, The Viking's Highland Lass, His

Wild Highland Lass (novella), Vexing the Highlander (novella), My Highlander

Other historical romances: Lady Caroline & the Egotistical Earl, A Ghost of a Chance at Love

* * *

Heart of the Wolf Series: Heart of the Wolf, Destiny of the Wolf, To Tempt the Wolf, Legend of the White Wolf, Seduced by the Wolf, Wolf Fever, Heart of the Highland Wolf, Dreaming of the Wolf, A SEAL in Wolf's Clothing, A Howl for a Highlander, A Highland Werewolf Wedding, A SEAL Wolf Christmas, Silence of the Wolf, Hero of a Highland Wolf, A Highland Wolf Christmas, A SEAL Wolf Hunting; A Silver Wolf Christmas, A SEAL Wolf in Too Deep, Alpha Wolf Need Not Apply, Billionaire in Wolf's Clothing, Between a Rock and a Hard Place, SEAL Wolf Undercover, Dreaming of a White Wolf Christmas, Flight of the White Wolf, All's Fair in Love and Wolf, A Billionaire Wolf for Christmas, SEAL Wolf Surrender (2019), Silver Town Wolf: Home for the Holidays (2019), Wolff Brothers: You Had Me at Wolf, Night of the Billionaire Wolf, Joy to the Wolves (Red Wolf), The Wolf Wore Plaid, Jingle Bell Wolf, Best of Both Wolves, While the Wolf's Away

SEAL Wolves: To Tempt the Wolf, A SEAL in Wolf's Clothing, A SEAL Wolf Christmas, A SEAL Wolf Hunting, A SEAL Wolf in Too Deep, SEAL Wolf Undercover, SEAL Wolf Surrender (2019)

Silver Bros Wolves: Destiny of the Wolf, Wolf Fever, Dreaming of the Wolf, Silence of the Wolf, A Silver Wolf Christmas, Alpha Wolf Need Not Apply, Between a Rock and a Hard Place, All's Fair in Love and Wolf, Silver Town Wolf: Home for the Holidays

Wolff Brothers of Silver Town Wolff Brothers: You Had Me at Wolf

Arctic Wolves: Legend of the White Wolf, Dreaming of a White Wolf Christmas, Flight of the White Wolf, While the Wolf's Away

Billionaire Wolves: Billionaire in Wolf's Clothing, A Billionaire Wolf for Christmas, Night of the Billionaire Wolf

Highland Wolves: Heart of the Highland Wolf, A Howl for a Highlander,

A Highland Werewolf Wedding, Hero of a Highland Wolf, A Highland Wolf Christmas, The Wolf Wore Plaid,

Red Wolf Series: Seduced by the Wolf, Joy to the Wolves, Best of Both Wolves,

* * *

Heart of the Jaguar Series: Savage Hunger, Jaguar Fever, Jaguar Hunt, Jaguar Pride, A Very Jaguar Christmas, You Had Me at Jaguar

Novella: The Witch and the Jaguar

Dawn of the Jaguar

* * *

Romantic Suspense: Deadly Fortunes, In the Dead of the Night, Relative Danger, Bound by Danger

* * *

Vampire romances: Killing the Bloodlust, Deadly Liaisons, Huntress for Hire, Forbidden Love, Vampire Redemption, Primal Desire

Vampire Novellas: Vampiric Calling, The Siren's Lure, Seducing the Huntress

* * *

Other Romance: Exchanging Grooms, Marriage, Las Vegas Style

* * *

Science Fiction Romance: Galaxy Warrior

Teen/Young Adult/Fantasy Books

The World of Fae:

The Dark Fae, Book 1

The Deadly Fae, Book 2

The Winged Fae, Book 3

The Ancient Fae, Book 4

Dragon Fae, Book 5

Hawk Fae, Book 6

Phantom Fae, Book 7

Golden Fae, Book 8

Falcon Fae, Book 9

Woodland Fae, Book 10

Angel Fae, Book 11

The World of Elf:

The Shadow Elf

Darkland Elf

Blood Moon Series:

Kiss of the Vampire

The Vampire...In My Dreams

Demon Guardian Series:

The Trouble with Demons

Demon Trouble, Too

Demon Hunter

Non-Series for Now:

Ghostly Liaisons

The Beast Within

Courtly Masquerade

Deidre's Secret

The Magic of Inherian:

The Scepter of Salvation

The Mage of Monrovia

Emerald Isle of Mists